Praise for

Bodyguards in Love

Brier's Bargain: Brier's Bargain is 100%, certifiably a must own, must read novel...This is a five star masterpiece that you will want to read over and over again, as long as you remember the tissues
~ *eCata Reviews*

Brier's Bargain: Thanks go to Ms. Lynne for an incredible story with real-to-life characters who come to life for the reader
~ *Fallen Angels Reviews*

Brier's Bargain is a touching story of love, promises, survival and about being the best that you are able to be. It is about hope and understanding and overcoming the past while looking towards the future. Wonderful read ~ *Night Owl Romance*

Seb's Surrender I enjoy how characters from the earlier book are continued and developed in the next book in the series. I loved watching as Jared's personality and trust emerged in spite of the terrible past he endured. I will be waiting for the next instalment in the Bodyguards in Love series. Thanks go to Ms. Lynne for a great read ~ *Fallen Angels Reviews*

Carol Lynne proves that literary gay sex does not have to be rough to be exciting, and that love is a universal turn-on
~ *Author, Lisabet Sarai*

BODYGUARDS IN LOVE
Volume One

Brier's Bargain

Seb's Surrender

CAROL LYNNE

Bodyguards in Love: Volume One
ISBN # 978-0-85715-059-2
©Copyright Carol Lynne 2010
Cover Art by Natalie Winters ©Copyright 2010
Interior text design by Claire Siemaszkiewicz
Total-E-Bound Publishing

Published in 2010 by Total-E-Bound Publishing, Think Tank, Ruston Way, Lincoln, LN6 7FL, United Kingdom.

BRIER'S
BARGAIN

Dedication

Thanks to all the Men in Love readers for their continued support. Hopefully, this new series will live up to that one.

Chapter One

"…DEFG…" Brier placed the last file in the appropriate spot and closed the drawer. "Do you have anything else for me to do, Sheila?"

"No, sweetie, you're all done. Why don't you see if Bram is ready to call it a day?" the accounting office secretary said with a smile.

"Okay. See you Monday." Brier picked up his coat and started to leave, but Sheila called him back.

"Brier? You forgot your paycheque."

Smiling, Brier turned and picked his cheque up from the table where he'd laid it earlier. "I'm gonna need this, too."

"Yeah? Special plans this weekend?"

"The carnival's in town. Bram and Declan promised to take me."

"Oh, isn't that nice. You have fun."

"I will." With one last grin, Brier went to find his twin brother. Since being released from the psychiatric hospital nearly three years ago, Brier had worked and lived with Bram and his partner Declan.

He knew Bram was taking him to the carnival to help get his mind off of Jackie. Brier stopped walking and rubbed his eyes. Thinking about the only man he'd ever truly been in love with still made his chest hurt. Jackie had said he loved Brier too, but then Jackie had gone away to some foreign country and left him all alone.

Brier knew it was Jackie's job to go train bodyguards for Three Partner's Protection Agency, the company they all worked for, but it didn't make it any easier to be alone. He waved hi to Mac as he passed his office on the way to Bram's.

He poked his head in and smiled. "You almost finished?"

Bram looked up from his computer, those little tiny reading glasses perched on the end of his nose that Brier thought made his brother look so smart. "Yep. Just give me another ten minutes or so."

"Okay. I'm gonna see if Mac's going to the carnival."

Bram nodded and went back to his computer. Brier travelled back down the hall to Mac's office. He leaned against the doorjamb and waited for Mac to notice him.

"Hey," Mac greeted. "How was your day?"

"Good. I got everything filed that Sheila asked me to, and I finished painting the break-room."

"I know. The break-room looks terrific. I'm glad you suggested we go with the yellow. It really livens it up."

Brier felt a blush creep up his cheeks. Mac always said nice things to him, but it was still hard for Brier to take a compliment without getting embarrassed. "Are you going to the carnival?"

Mac smiled and leaned back in his chair. "No, I think we'll skip it this year. You?"

"Yeah. Bram and Declan are taking me." Brier held up his paycheque. "Except I'm paying for myself."

"That's good."

Brier tapped his foot on the leg of the desk. He wanted to ask a question, but didn't want Mac to get mad at him.

"Something wrong, Brier?"

Brier shook his head. "I was just wondering if you'd talked to Jackie? He hasn't called me for a while."

Mac looked uneasy for a moment before his attention shifted to the door. Brier looked over his shoulder at Bram. "You ready?" Bram asked.

"Yeah. I was just asking Mac if he'd talked to Jackie."

Bram took a deep breath. "I imagine Jackie's too busy to call anyone these days. Don't take it personally, brother."

Brier stood and stuffed his cheque back into his coat pocket. He had a feeling something was going on. For several days he'd caught Bram whispering to Declan. A couple of times Brier thought he heard Jackie's name, but when he questioned Bram, his brother always denied it. Maybe Jackie wasn't coming home. What if he fell in love with someone else and didn't want Brier anymore?

He felt that throbbing thing start in his head again. Brier lifted his hand to the thick scar on the side of his skull to rub away the pain, but it didn't help. The scar his father had given to him as a baby was a constant reminder that he'd never be as smart as his twin brother. How a father could abuse an infant and then just sign over custody to the state when that abuse had permanent repercussions, Brier still didn't understand. At least he was happy his father had been convicted after abuse led to the paralysis of his younger brother Thor. Brier didn't feel a bit sorry that his father had been murdered in prison. He began to rub harder at the raised scar that ran in a large arc above his right ear.

"You okay?" Bram asked, stepping into the office.

"Head hurts."

"Did you take your medicine?"

Brier hated it when Bram tried to baby him. He wasn't a baby. "Yes. It just hurts sometimes when I get upset." He pushed past Bram to the hall. "See you Monday, Mac. If you talk to Jackie, tell him I said hi."

Bram stayed in Mac's office for a few more minutes. Brier decided not to wait on him and went out to stand by Bram's car. It was hot outside, so Brier took off his jacket. He thought it was weird how the mornings could be cold, but then the afternoons would get so hot.

Bram finally came out of the building and unlocked the doors. "I guess I should've given you the keys. You could've started the air conditioning."

Brier didn't say much. He got in and fastened his seat belt before leaning his head against the window. The hot glass felt good as it rubbed on the scar. "Are we going to eat at the carnival?"

"Whatever you want. This is your night." Bram pulled out of the parking lot and headed for home.

Brier turned to his brother. Bram had been very patient with him since Jackie left. He hated that he'd had the meltdown while staying at the Triple Spur. Ever since that night, Bram had treated him differently. The way he'd been treated when he'd first been released from the psychiatric hospital in Oklahoma.

The hospital reminded him of Carl, Jimmy and Rick, the men who'd sexually abused him in the hospital. Bram had told him that Carl and Jimmy were in a little trouble, but they wouldn't be going to jail, and the police hadn't found Rick yet. He'd moved away. "Have you heard anything about Rick?"

Bram got a surprised look on his face. "What brought that up?"

Brier shrugged. "I don't know, just thinking about stuff."

"Sounds like some pretty heavy thinking."

"Maybe," Brier mumbled.

"The police haven't located Rick yet, but when they do, they want to put him in jail."

"Because of me?"

"Because of what he's done to several men in the hospitals he's worked in." Bram shifted in his seat, and didn't look at Brier anymore. "They want you to testify, but I told them no."

"Why?" Brier asked.

"I don't think you're up to sitting in a courtroom with Rick, telling everyone in the room about the things he did to you."

Brier pressed his scar harder against the glass. "I don't wanna see him. He's scary."

Bram nodded and reached over to squeeze Brier's hand. "I know, buddy. That's why I told the police they'd have to find another way to convict him."

Brier felt better. At least Rick couldn't get to him if he didn't see him. Rick used to tell him he'd kill him if he ever told. Brier knew he'd do it to. Rick was a bad, bad man.

"I have money to buy us all corndogs for supper," he said, trying to change the subject.

"Are you sure that's what you want to do with your paycheque? I can buy my own dinner."

"You buy me dinner all the time."

"Okay. Corndogs it is."

* * * *

Brier felt a lot better by the time they arrived at the carnival. He got out of the car and looked around. There was so much going on. He didn't know what to look at first. "I want to ride that," he announced, pointing towards the Ferris wheel.

Bram chuckled. "I think we should save that one for after we eat. Let's try one of the more adventurous rides first."

Brier took off towards the rides. He remembered from the previous year that he had to buy tickets in order to ride. He dug his wallet out of his back pocket and counted out some money. "Do you want me to buy your tickets, too?" he asked Declan and Bram.

"We'll get our own," Declan said, pulling out some money.

Reading the note on the front of the ticket window, Brier tried to figure out how many he needed. He glanced over his shoulder at Declan. "How many are you getting?"

Declan reached past him and pointed towards the third option down on the list. "I think this one will do just fine for me and Bram, but maybe you should get this one."

Brier nodded and counted out enough money before stepping into line. He wanted to go in the Fun House for sure. Those goofy mirrors always made him laugh. Once it was his turn, he handed his money over to the guy behind the glass. "Tickets, please."

The guy gave him a bracelet instead of tickets. Confused, Brier held his money back out of the man's reach. "Don't I get tickets?"

"You had a twenty in your hand, I thought you wanted the bracelet," the guy droned.

Declan cut in front of Brier and spoke to the ticket guy. "He does. I'll explain it to him." Declan took the money out of Brier's hand and gave it to the guy behind the glass.

Brier watched Declan give the guy money for actual tickets. Now he was really confused. When Declan led him away from the booth, Brier questioned him. "Why do you get tickets, and I only get this silly paper bracelet for my money?"

Declan smiled and took the bracelet from Brier. "Because with this, you can ride as many rides as you want. It's a better deal for you." Declan fastened the bracelet around Brier's wrist.

"So why didn't you and Bram get one?"

"Because we don't like to ride as much as you do, so it wouldn't have been worth the money for us."

Brier nodded like he understood, but he really didn't. Money still tended to confuse him. He knew he was getting better. Bram had already started a savings account with the money he earned at his job. He was

saving up to buy a car. Bram had promised to take him
to get his driver's licence as soon as the doctor cleared it.
Sometimes he worried that he should spend his money
and get an apartment to live in like most men his age,
but Bram and Declan kept telling him they enjoyed
having him around.

"What's first?" Bram asked when they rejoined him.

Brier looked around. He knew he wanted to ride all of
them, so he decided to let Bram pick first. "Whatever
you want."

Bram headed towards the Tilt-A-Whirl. Brier grinned.
He loved that one. Everyone always got all smushed
together. As they waited in line, Brier turned to Declan.
"So what do I give the guy when I get up there?"

Declan gave him a friendly pat on the back. "Nothing,
just show him your bracelet."

"Wow. Cool." He liked the bracelet thing already.
Usually he ended up dropping half his tickets on the
ground when he dug them out of his pocket.

Brier flashed his bracelet with a smile when it was
their turn. He chose one of the little sea-shell-shaped
cars that was already a little tilty. "This one looks
good."

"Hmmm, the big question is who sits where," Bram
said.

"Declan in the middle since he's the smallest," Brier
replied, getting in.

After the guy came around to make sure everything
was locked down tight, the ride began. Brier leaned to
the side, hoping to make the car spin. He noticed a little
resistance from Declan, but Bram helped him out by

leaning into Declan. Their little sea shell started spinning really fast, and Declan began to groan.

Brier couldn't keep from laughing. He loved the way the spins made his tummy feel. By the time the ride slowed to a stop, Brier was ready to go again, but Bram had to help Declan off the ride and down the steps. "Are you okay?"

Declan took a handkerchief out of his pocket and wiped his forehead. "Just a little dizzy."

Brier felt bad that he'd made Declan go on the ride. "Should we go sit down?"

Declan shook his head. "Why don't you go on one, and Bram and I'll watch."

"Okay." Brier bounced a little as he tried to decide on which ride to choose. He saw one that went upside down. "Ooh, that one." He pointed.

Bram laughed and rolled his eyes. "Better you than me."

There were a couple of chairs close to the ride, so Bram made Declan sit down. "You go ahead. We'll watch from here."

Brier nodded and got in line, happy to have his bracelet. The line was really long which told him it must be a really good ride. He was looking up at the small cages as they spun around and upside down when someone slapped him on the shoulder.

"Hey, Brier."

Brier glanced over and saw Charlie and another guy from Three Partners that he'd seen in the halls. "Hi, Charlie. You gonna ride this?"

"Yeah." Charlie removed his hand and scratched the back of his neck. "Listen. I just wanted to say how sorry I am about what happened to Jackie."

"Huh?"

"Don't worry though. I'm sure he'll pull through. Jackie's one of the toughest sonofabitches I know. No way a little bomb could keep him down."

Brier's mouth filled with saliva. *Uh oh*. He covered his mouth and ran to the nearest trash can before he threw up. He heard Charlie and Bram arguing behind him as he continued to spew what little was left in his stomach.

All he could think about was Jackie and the word bomb. He'd seen bombs on TV and knew it was bad, really bad. Brier wiped his mouth and turned around to face his brother. He could tell by Bram's expression that he already knew about Jackie and the bomb. How could his brother have kept something like this from him? The days of not getting a phone call from Jackie suddenly made sense. Bram kept telling him Jackie must be busy when all the time he knew the truth.

Brier went from sick, to heartbroken, to pissed in about sixty seconds. Without saying a word, he reared back and punched his brother in the face, feeling the satisfying crunch as his fist connected with Bram's nose.

Without looking back, Brier turned and started running. He needed to talk to Mac. His boss would be able to tell him where Jackie was. All Brier wanted was to find Jackie and make him better.

He pushed his way through the crowd to the main street of town. After running several blocks, he stopped and tried to figure out where he was. Since the office for

Three Partners was also Mac's home, he knew the address. He saw a cab and waved down the driver.

Getting into the backseat, Brier gave the older man the address before digging out his wallet. He'd never taken a taxi by himself, but he'd been with Bram and Declan several times when they'd taken a cab. The car pulled up outside Three Partners and he gave the driver some money, making sure he gave him a few extra dollars for a tip.

He ran up the front steps and rang the doorbell. After a few seconds, he looked through the stained glass panel beside the door and pounded on the heavy wood. He saw Nicco running towards him.

The door opened and Nicco pulled him inside and hugged him. "I'm so glad you're here. Bram called. He's worried sick about you."

"I don't want to talk about him. I want to know about Jackie. I need to find him. Will you help me?"

"Come on," Nicco said, leading Brier to the living quarters.

Mac and Amir were both on the phone when Nicco sat with him on the couch. "Amir is talking to Bram, and Mac is finding out the latest on Jackie. He knew you'd want to know."

Brier's heart plummeted. So, everyone knew about Jackie but him. He felt his eyes sting as the tears he'd tried so hard to hold back, dripped down his face. He didn't bother wiping them away, the way he felt, there wouldn't be any stopping them anyway. He felt completely betrayed by the people who said they loved him.

Picking up a pillow from the couch, Brier buried his face in it, shrugging loose of Nicco's hand on his shoulder.

"Declan's taking Bram by the ER to get his nose set before they come over," Amir's accented voice said.

Maybe eventually Brier would feel guilty about punching Bram, but not right now. He wished he could just go to the emergency room and have his pain taken away. Pulling the pillow away from his face he looked at Nicco. "Is Jackie gonna die?"

Nicco glanced at the other men in the room before turning to Brier. "They don't think so, but he was hurt really bad."

"Can you take me to him?" Brier asked, the tears still sliding down his face.

"No. He's in a hospital in Jurru. Do you know where that is?"

Brier nodded. "Bram showed me on a map, but why can't you take me there?"

Nicco ran his fingers through his hair. "Because you probably wouldn't be able to see him anyway and you don't have a passport."

"Well get me one," Brier demanded.

"I can't."

Mac hung up the phone and sat on the coffee table in front of Brier. "I just talked to the hospital in Jurru. Jackie's still in a drug induced coma, but they say his vital signs appear to be improving."

"Why? What happened to him? How come no one told me?" Brier had so many questions that he didn't know where to start.

Mac reached for Brier's hand. "There was an attempt on Prince Zahar's life. One of his servants was killed and Jackie was injured when a car bomb exploded in front of the palace as the Prince was coming out to get into his car."

Brier knew Jackie must be hurt really bad by the way Mac was talking to him. "Is he gonna die?"

Mac shook his head. "I don't think so, but it's still a little early to tell." Mac rubbed the back of his neck, obviously struggling with what he was about to say. "Jackie lost his left leg from the knee down. He also suffered some internal injuries, but the doctors think they either fixed or removed everything that was damaged. They're worried about infection. That's what's happening inside Jackie's body right now."

"What can I do?" Brier asked.

"The only thing any of us can do is pray," Nicco said, hugging Brier from the side.

"Okay." Brier stood and turned towards the door.

"Where are you going?" Mac asked.

"To the church down the street," Brier informed them. He was thankful he'd been given something to do that would help the man he loved.

When Brier arrived at the church, he was sad to find the doors locked. He stood on the steps for a few moments before sitting down. *I guess this is as close as I can get, God. I hope you can still hear me.*

Brier talked to God until a car pulled up to the curb in front of him. Bram and Declan got out and walked towards him. "You okay?" Brier asked, taking in the bandage across the bridge of his brother's nose.

"I'm fine," Bram said, and sat down next to Brier.

"Sorry," Brier apologised, unable to meet Bram's eyes.

"I deserved it. I should've told you about Jackie."

"He'll be okay now. I had a long talk with God, and he's going to make Jackie all better," Brier informed Bram and Declan.

"Good. Then all of this was worth it."

Brier nodded. "Please don't keep things from me. I think sometimes you forget that I'm a couple of minutes older than you are."

Bram chuckled and gave Brier a hug. "You know, I think you're right. I'll do better, I promise."

Chapter Two

Over the next several days Brier prayed every chance he was given. He spent every lunch hour as well as before and after work at the church he'd visited that first night. Finishing up his daily filing, he was interrupted by a big hug from Bram.

"Good news. Jackie's awake and doing well."

Brier turned and wrapped his arms around his brother. "It worked. When can he come home?"

Bram shook his head. "Not for a little while yet. The doctors need to make sure he's strong enough to make the long flight. Don't worry though. Prince Zahara offered his private plane and while in Jurru, the Prince is seeing to it that Jackie has everything he needs."

"Except for me," Brier mumbled. "So how long do you think?"

"A week. Maybe ten days. Of course when he gets back to the States he'll need around the clock supervision. The Prince asked me to arrange a nurse to care for his wounds so he could recuperate at home."

"He doesn't need a nurse. I can do it."

Bram smiled and hugged Brier tighter. "You can visit all you want, but Jackie's going to need special care. His leg will need constant attention to make sure infection doesn't set in again."

"I can learn how to do that."

"I'm sorry, but he really does need a nurse."

God, he hated being stupid. Brier didn't want to do anything to hurt Jackie, so he eventually nodded. "Can I at least stay at his house with him? That way the nurse doesn't have to sleep there."

Bram patted him on the back. "That sounds like a damn good idea, brother. We'll see how Jackie feels about it. The main reason I came in here was because Jackie asked to speak with you. What do you say we go into my office and give him a call?"

"Really?" Without waiting for Bram, Brier broke away and ran to his brother's office. He had the phone in his hand when Bram finally walked into the room. Laughing, Bram took the phone from Brier and dialled. He had to go through several people before he was connected to Jackie.

"Hey, buddy, how're you feeling?

Brier paced back and forth, biting on his thumbnail while Bram talked to Jackie for a few minutes. He knew he had to rush over to the church as soon as he finished talking to Jackie. He had someone to thank and didn't think it should wait.

Bram grinned at Brier. "Listen, I've got someone here who's fixing to bite off his thumb if I don't let him talk to you. You up for it?" Bram chuckled and held the phone out to Brier.

Grabbing the cordless phone, Brier walked towards the corner of the room. "Jackie?"

"Hey, sweetheart." Jackie's voice sounded really different to Brier.

"Are you okay?" Brier asked.

"No, but I'm getting there. They tell me I'll be home in another week or so. I can't wait to see you."

"I've been praying," Brier admitted. "I knew you'd be okay."

There was silence for several moments before Jackie spoke. "Listen, sweetheart. I'm not the same man that you're used to."

"Because of what happened to your leg?"

"Yeah. That and I've got a few new scars. I hope I don't scare you when you finally see me."

Brier shook his head. "You won't. I love you. I just want you to come home so I can take care of you."

Jackie sighed. "Are you sure you want to do that? Depending on my recovery, it could be a long time before I'm able to make love to you."

"That's okay. Will I still get those kisses I like so much?"

Jackie laughed and then started coughing. "Don't make me laugh, it hurts," Jackie continued to chuckle.

"I'm sorry." He hadn't meant to make Jackie hurt. Brier hoped his boyfriend would forgive him.

"No, don't be sorry. Talking to you is the only thing that could possibly make me smile these days. And to answer your question, yes. You'll get more than enough kisses from me."

Jackie started to sound tired. Brier knew it was time to hang up, but it seemed he'd waited so long to hear his Jackie's voice he hated to. "I miss you. I miss your kisses."

"Me too, sweetheart. I'll see you soon though. I love you," Jackie said with a yawn.

"Get some rest and get better. Do what the doctors tell you to do so you can come back home."

"I promise. Will you call me every day?"

"I'd like that very much. It's lonely not talking to you at night."

"Just hang on and before you know it, you'll have me every night."

"I'm counting on it." Brier hung up the phone and turned back to Bram. "Do we have time for me to go to church before we go home?"

"Sure," Bram said with a nod.

* * * *

It ended up being almost two full weeks before Jackie was flown home. Bram took Brier to the executive airport to meet the Prince's plane. "I can't believe how jumpy my stomach feels," Brier said.

"Just nerves. It'll settle down once you see Jackie again," Bram soothed, petting Brier's hair.

With his forehead pressed to the wall of glass, Brier watched as a big man carried Jackie down the aeroplane's steps to a waiting wheelchair. It was the first look he'd had of the man he loved in a long time. Brier pounded on the window, trying to get Jackie's attention.

"He can't hear you," Bram told him. "It's noisy out on the runway."

Brier watched as Jackie disappeared somewhere underneath the window. "Where'd he go?"

"They'll bring him up the elevator." Bram pointed towards the big stainless steel doors. Brier rushed over and stood, waiting.

When he heard the subtle ding of the elevator arriving on the floor, his forehead broke out into a cold sweat. When the doors whooshed open, Brier held his breath, waiting for a sign from Jackie. Not wanting Jackie to feel bad, Brier didn't look down at his leg.

Brier was met by his lover's big smile as the man with muscles pushed Jackie's wheelchair out of the elevator. Jackie opened his arms and beckoned Brier. "Don't I get a hug?"

Releasing the breath he'd been holding, Brier started to run into Jackie's arms. "Be careful!" Bram admonished.

Oh, yeah. Brier slowed and knelt beside Jackie. He almost cooed when Jackie's arms surrounded him. Brier rested his head on Jackie's shoulder and sent a quick 'thank you' up to God. "I'm so happy you're home."

Jackie lifted Brier's chin and kissed him. "I've needed that," Jackie said, pulling back from the kiss. "I hear you're planning to help take care of me."

Brier nodded enthusiastically. "If you'll let me."

"Of course I'll let you." Jackie looked over his shoulder at the silent man. He said something in a language Brier didn't understand, but he heard the name Malik. The big guy shook Jackie's hand and turned to get back on the elevator.

"Who was that?" Brier asked, as he began pushing the wheelchair to the parking lot.

"Malik. He's one of Prince Zahar's trusted friends."

By the time Brier got Jackie settled in the backseat, Bram arrived with Jackie's luggage. Brier shut Jackie's door and walked to the trunk to stand beside Bram. "Is it okay if I sit in back?"

Bram grinned. "I'd worry if you wanted to sit anywhere else."

Brier got in and slid next to Jackie. "Bram took me grocery shopping and we bought stuff I know how to cook."

"You're going to do some more cooking for me? You know how sexy I think that is."

Brier felt his face heat. "Yeah," he mumbled, picking at a hole in the knee of his jeans. He remembered what both Jackie and Bram had told him. He shook his finger at his boyfriend. "But no funny business until the doctor says so."

Jackie chuckled and pulled Brier in for a deep kiss. Brier felt Jackie's tongue invade his mouth and moaned. He could feel his cock growing within the confines of the old denim he wore. "You're not making it any easier," he laughed, looking down at the fly of his jeans.

Jackie leaned closer and whispered in Brier's ear. "I may not be up for fucking, but I can sure as hell take care of that problem of yours when we get home."

Brier's eyes widened in surprise, he loved it when Jackie sucked on his cock. "Okay," he whispered back. He ran his tongue over the shell of Jackie's ear and was rewarded with a groan.

Shocked, Brier looked towards Bram to see if his brother had heard. He watched Bram's eyes crinkle at the corners as his brother smiled. Brier decided to be good for the rest of the ride home. Although he didn't move out of Jackie's arms, he laid his head on his lover's chest. The position gave him time to look at Jackie's leg. It looked odd to Brier. The way the bottom of Jackie's pants was pinned up you could tell where the leg had been severed just below the knee.

"Does it bother you?" Jackie asked.

Ashamed of himself for looking, Brier shook his head. "No." He tentatively reached down and ran his fingers over the ball-looking thing. "What's this?"

"Bandages. They'll come off once the nurse arrives at my house. The doctor in Jurru put this big one on for the trip. Would you like to watch the nurse take it off?"

"Will it hurt?" He knew he couldn't watch Jackie in pain.

"No. I'd like you to be there. I need you to know exactly what you're getting in to."

"Okay. Maybe she can show me how to do it."

Jackie kissed the top of Brier's head. "Maybe."

* * * *

Despite what Jackie had told him in the car, Brier tucked his lover into bed. "You need to sleep, and I need to make us some dinner."

To his surprise, Jackie nodded. "Can you do me a favour and bring me my medicine? It's in the zippered kit inside my suitcase."

Brier noticed how pale Jackie had become since arriving at his house. "Are you hurting?"

"Just a little," Jackie said. Brier could tell by the way Jackie said it that he was in more pain then he'd let on.

Rushing over to the suitcase, Brier rummaged around until he found the leather bag. He carried it over to the bed and unzipped it. "Wow." He couldn't believe how many bottles of pills were inside. Brier began lining them all up on the bedside table. "Which ones?"

Jackie pointed to one of the bottles. "Those. Can you get me out two of them, and I'll also need a glass of water?"

Brier had a hard time opening the bottle at first. He finally got it open and shook out two tiny tablets. After handing them to Jackie, he rushed to the kitchen for a glass of water.

By the time he arrived back in the bedroom, Jackie had already swallowed the pills. Jackie reached out and took the water. "Thanks." Brier watched as Jackie drank the entire glass before handing it back. Jackie closed his eyes and seemed to sink back into his pillows. "So what're you making me for dinner?" he asked, without opening his eyes.

"Does grilled cheese sandwiches and tomato soup sound okay?" He wished he could make better things but that was one of the few menu items he was allowed to cook.

"Mmm, sounds like just what I need at the moment."

Brier sat on the edge of the bed and feathered his fingers through Jackie's blond hair. "It doesn't take very long. Should I wait until you're done with your nap?"

Jackie opened his eyes and smiled. Brier thought the smile appeared a tad forced. "Go ahead and make it. I'm supposed to eat something with the pain meds. Just wake me up when it's ready."

"Okay." Brier gave Jackie a brief kiss before getting up. "Holler if you need anything."

"I will," Jackie mumbled, his eyes closing again.

Brier looked down at the man he loved for several moments before going into the kitchen. As he got out the supplies he'd need, he began to wonder if he'd be able to take care of Jackie the way he would need. Maybe he could ask Lilly or Declan to teach him a few more things to cook? That would help. Right?

He opened the can of soup and realised he didn't know what to put in it. He reached for the phone and called Declan.

"Hello?"

"Hey."

"Hi, Brier. How're things going with your patient?" Declan sounded concerned, and Brier wanted to put his mind at ease.

"Jackie's took some pain pills and he's taking a nap while I make dinner, but I have a question."

"Okay."

"I can't remember if I should put milk in the tomato soup or water," Brier admitted.

"Technically, either is fine, but I like to make it with half a can of water and fill it the rest of the way with milk."

"Right," Brier said, nodding his head. "I guess that's what got me confused. Okay. Thanks."

"Brier?"

"Yeah?"

"If you need anything at all, call us. Don't be afraid to ask for help when you need it."

Brier felt his eyes burn at the love and acceptance he heard in Declan's voice. "I will, promise." Brier hung up and dried his eyes, ashamed at himself for getting too emotional. "Jackie needs a man right now so stop being a baby," he told himself.

With the tray of food in hand, Brier walked into the bedroom. Jackie was still sleeping. *That's good.* Before he could wake Jackie, the doorbell rang. "Shoot," Brier said, setting the food on the bedside table.

He left the room without waking Jackie and answered the door. A middle-aged woman smiled at him. "Hi, I'm Dana. The visiting nurse," she further clarified.

"Oh, hi." Brier shook Dana's hand. "I'm Brier, Jackie's boyfriend." He stepped back enough to let Dana inside. "He's asleep."

"How's he feeling?"

Brier bit his lip. He wasn't sure if he should tell Dana what Jackie obviously didn't want him to know. In the end, he decided the important thing was making Jackie better. "I think he hurts, but he won't tell me. He took two pain pills after we got him in bed."

Dana nodded and gave Brier's arm a pat. "He's probably afraid to worry you. It's fairly common so don't take it personally. Men want to pretend they're too tough to be in pain." Dana grinned. "Either that, or they're the world's biggest babies. Sounds like your Jackie falls into the first category."

"I made him some dinner, but he hasn't gotten a chance to eat it yet. He told me he needed something after taking the pills."

"Well then, we'll just have to let him eat before I assess his condition."

Brier smiled. He liked this woman. "Come on. He's back here." Brier led Dana to the master bedroom. "Jackie? It's time to wake up and eat something." Jackie didn't stir and Brier started to worry. He looked over his shoulder at Dana.

Dana motioned for Brier to give Jackie a shake. Reaching down, Brier put his hand on Jackie's shoulder and applied a little pressure, afraid he'd do something to hurt his lover. "Jackie? Your nurse is here. Time to wake up."

Jackie's eyes fluttered for a few moments before opening. Brier leant down and kissed his forehead. "This is Dana. She's here to make sure you're getting better, but first you need to eat your supper."

After rubbing his eyes, Jackie looked at Dana. "It's nice to meet you."

"Do you need help sitting up? You really should eat," Dana advised.

Brier watched as Jackie pushed himself up with his arms, but he seemed to struggle to get back to the headboard. Reaching out, Brier hooked his hands under Jackie's armpits and lifted him into position.

Jackie whistled. "Someone's gotten stronger," he teased Brier.

Brier shrugged. He didn't want to tell Jackie in front of Dana that working out helped him control his mood swings. Instead, he lifted the tray and set it on Jackie's lap. "I hope it's still warm. Let me know because I can always put it in the microwave."

Jackie dipped the corner of his sandwich into the bowl of soup. "Mmm," he groaned after taking a bite. "This is really good."

Brier felt his chest puff out a little at the compliment. It made him feel good to know he'd made Jackie happy. "I can make you another sandwich if you want?"

Jackie swallowed his bite of food. "No. This'll be perfect. I'm not used to eating so well. I think my stomach has shrunk."

Brier gently sat on the edge of the mattress, making sure not to upset Jackie's tray. Jackie finished off his sandwich and picked up the spoon to eat the rest of his soup. "Did you eat?" Jackie asked.

Brier shook his head. "Not yet, but I will. I wanted to get you taken care of first."

Jackie ended up drinking the rest of the soup directly from the bowl. When he pulled the dish from his lips, he had a cute little red moustache. Brier couldn't help giggling. He pulled a napkin from the tray and wiped Jackie's mouth. "You're silly."

Jackie smiled. "Good dinner, sweetheart. Thank you."

Brier stood and lifted the tray from Jackie's lap. "I'll take care of this while Dana does whatever she's gonna do."

Dana pulled the stethoscope from around her neck and put the ends into her ears, ready to start her exam. "You're going to come back when she removes the dressing aren't you?" Jackie asked, before Brier could leave the room.

"Yeah." Brier took the dishes into the kitchen and set them on the counter. He eyed the pot of soup and decided he'd better eat something. After Dana left, he was hoping to snuggle up with Jackie if he wasn't in too much pain. Instead of getting another bowl out of the cabinet, Brier lifted the soup pot and drank it like Jackie had. He felt a little guilty, knowing Bram would have a fit if he saw Brier doing it, but that made it even more fun.

By the time he arrived back in the bedroom, Dana had Jackie's clothes off. Brier looked from a nude Jackie to Dana. "What's going on?"

Jackie held out his hand and Brier took it, noticing the bright pink scars on his lover's body. "Don't worry. Dana's a nurse. She's just making sure nothing's infected."

"And everything looks like it should so far," Dana added, getting a pair of scissors out of her big bag. "I'm going to cut away these bandages. Would you like to help me?"

Brier nodded. Maybe if he learned how to change Jackie's dressing, Dana wouldn't need to see his boyfriend naked anymore. He watched closely as she snipped away the big ball of bandages.

"Sure you're ready to see this?" Jackie asked. "It's kinda gross looking."

"I'll be okay," Brier answered, refusing to look away from the task at hand.

When Dana pulled off the outer shell of bandages and then what she called a shrink bandage, Brier gasped. "It's all red."

"That's pretty natural," Dana informed him. "The skin is still healing."

Brier squeezed Jackie's hand. "Okay."

"Could you get me a warm wet washcloth? I think a spit-bath might make Jackie feel better."

Brier released Jackie's hand and went to the bathroom. As he ran water over the thick terrycloth, he noticed himself in the mirror. His bronzed skin was paler than usual and his face appeared a little pinched. Brier took several deep breaths, trying to calm himself before returning to Jackie's side. He knew if Jackie suspected this was upsetting Brier, he'd never send the nurse away. "You can do this," he told his reflection.

He returned to the bedroom and handed Dana the wet cloth. She placed it over the end of Jackie's stump and held it there for several moments. Brier looked at Jackie's face to make sure Dana wasn't hurting him.

"It's okay, sweetheart. I've been through this several times a day for the last month." Jackie tapped his lips with his finger. "But a little kiss sure wouldn't hurt."

Brier leant down and kissed his boyfriend. "I love you."

"I know you do. That's why I told the doctors I needed to get home. I couldn't have the man I love stewing over me."

"Okay, I think we're ready," Dana said, setting the washcloth aside.

The stump, as the nurse had referred to it, looked strange to him. Dana got into her bag and pulled out a bottle of clear liquid and some gauze pads. She soaked the pads and began gently cleaning the stump. There was a big scar, but Brier was pleased to see it looked like it was doing well. He'd had a cut that had gotten infected before, so at least he had an idea of what to look for.

"Looks good," Dana said. "I think you should be about ready to get fitted with your prosthetic limb. Have you been touching it? It'll be quite sensitive, but in order to help with the addition of the prosthesis, you'll need to get used to something touching it."

"I have," Jackie informed her. His gaze shot from Dana's to Brier's. "Uh, when do you think I can resume...intimate relations?"

Dana chuckled. "As soon as you feel up to it. Just be careful." Dana shook her head. "Most men have a hard time resuming sex after an amputation. Though it's usually due to depression more than anything."

Jackie shook his head. "I'm not most men. I'm thankful I lived. If the cost for surviving that blast was losing a leg, I consider myself lucky."

Dana reached out and patted Jackie's good leg. "Then you're definitely not most men. You've got a fantastic attitude. That's good because you're going to need it."

Brier watched Dana pick up the shrink bandage once again. "Do you want this on, or would you rather leave it off for a while?"

"Leave it off." Jackie glanced at Brier. "I think *we* need to get used to seeing it as it is."

Dana packed her bag and Brier saw her out. "Thanks for being patient with me," Brier told Dana. "I know you can probably tell I'm not as smart as most people, but I really love Jackie, and I want to help him get better."

Dana smiled. "I wish all my patients were lucky enough to have someone like you to look after them. And for the record, intelligence has little to do with it, having patience and compassion is the most important part."

Brier nodded. "I have those."

"I know. I can see it in your eyes when you look at him." Dana handed Brier a white business card. "Don't be afraid to call me with any questions."

"Thanks." Brier closed and locked the door. He walked around the house and turned off all the lights before retreating back to the bedroom. Jackie was once again asleep when he entered.

Brier quietly got undressed and turned off the overhead light before sliding under the covers. Jackie mumbled something that Brier couldn't understand and pulled Brier against his side. Brier draped his arm over Jackie's chest, making sure not to hurt him and snuggled in. He was asleep within moments.

Chapter Three

"I need you to do something for me," Jackie said.

Brier put down the breakfast tray and sat on the edge of the bed. "Do you need more pills?"

Shaking his head, Jackie reached out and pulled Brier against his nude chest. It had been three days since he'd been home and Brier was still treating him with kid gloves. "No. I feel great this morning. So good that I'd like for you to get back in bed with me."

Brier's dark brown eyes rounded in surprise. "Really?"

Jackie kissed him. The man in his arms had no idea just how much he was loved. Jackie had been honest when he'd told Dana he didn't begrudge his injury. It sucked, but it was what it was. While in the military, he'd seen first-hand what depression did to the strongest men. Jackie didn't plan on becoming a statistic.

In the past few days, he'd gotten Brier used to looking and lightly touching his stump. Now, he needed him to touch something else. As the kiss continued, he ran his hands down Brier's back to the bottom of his T-shirt and pulled it over his head. "Need to feel you."

Brier stood and started to undress. "What about your breakfast?"

"As good as those frozen waffles look, they aren't half as appetising as you." Jackie flipped back the covers on Brier's side of the bed. "I'm not sure how we're going to do this, but I need to make love to you."

Brier slid under the covers and ran his hand down Jackie's chest. "You'll tell me if anything hurts, right?"

Before he could answer, Brier leant down and took Jackie's nipple between his teeth, giving the protruding nub teasing bites. Jackie buried the fingers of one hand in Brier's hair, while smoothing his hand down Brier's spine with the other.

Brier must've known what Jackie was after and repositioned himself slightly, giving Jackie access to that sweet butt he loved so much. He palmed Brier's ass cheek and squeezed.

When Brier started to lick his way down Jackie's chest, he groaned. Giving Brier's ass a playful slap, he tugged on his lover's hip. "Swing your legs around here so I can taste you."

Grinning, Brier straddled Jackie's face, putting his ass and hard cock within reach. With so many choices, Jackie didn't know where to start. He finally sucked one of Brier's balls into his mouth, laving the slightly furry skin with his tongue.

"That feels good," Brier moaned, moments before engulfing Jackie's cock.

Jackie released Brier's testicle and chuckled. Making love to Brier was always a joy. His man was very vocal about what he liked and didn't like. Jackie's amusement was interrupted by Brier's swirling tongue against the sensitive skin of his shaft. It had been too long since he'd felt that beautifully warm mouth perform its tricks, and Jackie knew he wouldn't last long.

Instead of returning the favour, Jackie decided to concentrate on getting Brier's ass stretched and ready. He reached under his pillow for the tube of lube he'd tucked under there earlier. As he flipped open the top, he ran his tongue up the crease of Brier's crack from his sac to the sweetly puckered hole.

Brier released Jackie's cock. "Oh, yeah, right there. I've missed you doing that to me."

Jackie chuckled again and replaced his tongue with his lubed thumb. He applied pressure to the sensitive opening and waited for Brier's body to open up and accept the invasion. Brier didn't disappoint. Within minutes, Jackie had both thumbs inside his lover's heat.

Brier moved his ass from side to side, totally forgetting about sucking Jackie's cock. That was fine with Jackie. He wanted to come inside Brier's ass, not his mouth, and he was already so close to the edge, he was grinding his teeth.

Pulling away, Brier spun around and faced Jackie. "I need it now."

"Climb on," Jackie instructed, reaching out to pet Brier's cock.

Brier bit his lip and Jackie could see the indecision in his lover's eyes. "Don't worry. You're not going to hurt me." The fresh scars on his hip, thigh and groin were all but healed, but Jackie had a feeling he'd want inside Brier even if they weren't.

With a slight nod, Brier straddled Jackie's groin and guided himself down to the crown of Jackie's cock. "It's been a long time," Brier croaked, as Jackie's cock breeched his opening.

"Too long," Jackie agreed. He could tell by the rigid set of Brier's shoulders he needed a few seconds to acclimate his body's reaction to the invasion. "Hopefully we'll never have to be apart for that length of time again. I'm finished with field work."

Brier looked down at him with a hopeful expression. "Really?"

"Yep. Mac promised me a full-time job, training bodyguards. With the increased need for security specialists in the Middle East, Mac wants me to teach classes on customs and language."

"Remind me to give Mac a hug when I see him," Brier said, as he began to move up and down on Jackie's cock.

Jackie grunted, thrusting deeper inside Brier. He knew he'd never meet a more loyal lover, but the thought of Brier hugging anyone outside his family bugged him. "I think a handshake would do."

Brier's chuckle turned into a moan as he continued to fuck himself on Jackie's cock. Words were no longer necessary as they stared into each other's eyes. Jackie could see his own love reflected in the almost black eyes of his man. He ran his hands up Brier's muscular thighs to the tight six-pack his lover had further sculpted.

Brier's body was a thing of beauty. His thumbs travelled to the dark brown discs placed perfectly on Brier's chest. Circling the sensitive skin, he was rewarded with an all over body shiver.

"Pinch them," Brier groaned.

Taking the pebbled nubs between his thumbs and forefingers, Jackie did as asked. The aroused flesh hardened even further. "God, you're breathtaking," Jackie said in awe.

Brier reached down and wrapped a hand around his cock. "Wanna come," Brier announced.

"Do it, baby. Paint my chest." Jackie's sac drew up tight as the first strand of cum shot from Brier's cock. His lover's face had gone angelic as he continued to ride out his climax.

Jackie released Brier's nipples and slid his hands to his lover's shoulders. "Now," he groaned, pulling Brier down to bury himself as deep as possible in the gorgeous man's ass. Jackie's cock erupted, shooting his seed deep into Brier's ass.

Brier started to fall to Jackie's side, but Jackie wanted to feel the weight of his lover on his chest. He redirected Brier until the slightly smaller man was nestled in his arms. Jackie felt a bite of pain as Brier's body settled against the newly-healed abdominal scar, but it was worth it. Waking in the hospital, all Jackie could think about was making love to Brier again.

"I love you," Jackie said, kissing the top of Brier's head.

"I love you, too," Brier cooed.

* * * *

Brier knocked on Bram's office door. "Can I talk to you?"

"Sure," Bram replied, looking up from his computer. "How're things going with Jackie?"

"Really good. That's what I wanted to talk to you about. Jackie got fitted for his new leg a couple days ago."

"Good."

"Yeah, but he needs to go to therapy every day, and since I can't drive, we'll have to have someone take him."

"Not a problem. I'm sure we can have one of the guys drive over and pick him up."

Brier knew that would be Bram's reaction. Instead of continuing to beat around the bush he decided to tell his brother exactly what was on his mind. "I want you to talk to my doctor and teach me how to drive."

Bram's brows rose as he took off his reading glasses. "I thought we'd decided to give it another six months or so."

"We did, but that was before Jackie's injury. I can learn, Bram, I swear it."

Bram stood and walked around to lean against the front of his desk, directly in front of Brier. "I know you can learn, but we're worried because of all the medication you're on."

"I know that, but I don't need the meds anymore. Jackie makes me calm." Brier looked into eyes identical to his own. "Please. I want to take care of him on my own."

Bram sighed and pulled the thong out of his long, black braid. Brier knew it was a sure sign his brother was deep in thought. "I'll discuss it with Declan and your doctor."

Brier smiled. He wasn't offended Bram was going to talk to Declan. The two of them shared everything. "Thanks."

He started to leave, but stopped in the doorway, remembering what else he'd come in for. "Oh, I wanted to invite you and Declan over for dinner."

Bram chuckled. "You're really getting into this cooking thing, huh?"

"I like it. Jackie taught me how to make meatloaf."

"Mmm, you know that's one of my favourites," Bram groaned.

"Yep. Although I'm making instant mashed potatoes. I hope that's okay?"

"Sounds good. As far as I know Declan doesn't have anything planned, so I'm sure we'll be able to make it. What time?"

"Umm, six?"

Bram nodded and walked back around the desk. "We'll be there."

"And you'll call the doctor?" Brier prompted.

Bram appeared to study Brier for several moments. "Yeah."

"Thanks." Brier went back to the accounting office with a little skip in his step. He couldn't wait to get a driver's licence like most adults. He knew it was a small step, but it made him happy.

* * * *

Jackie placed the last of the biscuits on the cookie tray. "These are ready for the oven, but I wouldn't put them in until Bram and Declan get here."

Without saying a word, Brier put down the box of instant mashed potatoes and crossed the distance to the table. He started to take the sheet from Jackie's hand, but Jackie held on until Brier looked at him.

"What's going on?" Jackie asked.

Brier started to say something, but stopped, took a deep breath and smiled. "Nothing. I'm just scared. This is my first dinner party."

Damn his man was cute. Jackie looked around the kitchen. "Well, the meatloaf's in the oven, the table's been set and the rest of the stuff can be cooked once your guests arrive."

Jackie took the tray out of Brier's hand and pulled his lover onto his lap. "Relax."

"I know. I just want them to see how well I can take care of you," Brier mumbled.

"They'll be able to tell by the smile on my face." Jackie pointed towards his over-exaggerated smile.

Brier started laughing. "You're so funny."

Jackie hugged his lover tighter. What would he have done these past several weeks without Brier? He wondered if he'd ever be able to tell him what an inspiration he'd been. He hadn't told him, but Brier's determination to live a normal life despite his head injury was what had given Jackie the drive to persevere despite losing his lower leg.

Brier began placing angel kisses along the side of Jackie's head and neck. Jackie answered Brier's passion by unbuttoning his lover's shirt. Once Brier's bronzed muscled chest was exposed, Jackie couldn't keep his hands to himself. His fingers traced the dips in between the abdominal muscles before roaming up to circle and pinch Brier's dark brown nipples.

Brier moaned and moved to straddle Jackie's lap. "Touch me."

Now it was Jackie's turn to moan as Brier licked up the side of his face. Jackie reached between them and unfastened Brier's low-rise jeans, fishing out the dark-skinned cock he'd become obsessed with.

Brier's hips began to move, thrusting his length in and out of Jackie's tight grip. Brier was the most erotic, sensual man Jackie had ever had the good fortune to make love to, and they'd indulged almost non-stop since his return.

Fingernails scraped his flesh as Brier scrambled to pull up Jackie's shirt. The stinging sensation only added to Jackie's pleasure. With his other hand, Jackie pulled Brier in for a deep kiss. He thrust his tongue in Brier's mouth like he wanted to thrust into his lover's ass.

Jackie was about to suggest they get naked and fuck around the fancy dinnerware already set on the table, when the doorbell rang. "Fuck!"

Brier gazed into Jackie's eyes. "I need."

Knowing Bram and Declan were waiting, Jackie slipped a hand down the back of Brier's jeans. With one hand still jacking his lover, he pressed two fingers deep into Brier's still-stretched hole.

Back bowing, Brier grunted as he painted Jackie's fist and chest with seed. Once he'd milked his lover dry, Jackie removed his hands. "You know Bram will be barging in here any second, love. Best we clean up before that happens."

With a sly grin, Brier stood and went to the sink, wetting a dishtowel. He cleaned the drying cum from his cock while giving Jackie a particularly erotic show.

"You're killing me," Jackie moaned, pressing the heel of his hand against his still-trapped erection.

Brier chuckled and re-wet the cloth before kneeling in front of Jackie. Before wiping the seed from Jackie's chest, Brier scraped his teeth against the bulging fly of Jackie's jeans.

"As much as I want to tell you to keep going, I think I just heard the front door."

Brier's dark brown eyes rounded. He quickly cleaned Jackie's skin, and tossed the towel into the laundry room.

"We're in the kitchen," Jackie called while Brier zipped up.

Bram and Declan came through the swinging door with smiles on their faces. Bram went straight to the fridge and withdrew two cold beers, passing one to Declan. "We knew where you were. It was obvious by the moans."

Jackie winked at Brier who had gone red with embarrassment. Brier finally glanced at Bram. "Sorry."

Declan started to laugh. "Don't apologise. Bram's just jealous because we didn't have time before leaving the house."

Jackie didn't know that it was possible for Brier to go any redder. Deciding to take his lover's mind off the awkward situation, he cleared his throat. "Brier? Would you like to take the meatloaf out of the warmer and put the biscuits in?"

A relieved smile crossed Brier's gorgeous face as he grabbed the potholders and removed the baking dish from the oven. "I'll let that set while I make the rest of the food," Brier proclaimed.

With his nose in the air, Bram inhaled. "Mmm mmm, brother. That smells good."

"I chopped the bell peppers and onions in tiny pieces like you like them," Brier informed Bram.

Jackie crossed his arms, smiling at Bram. It was nice to see the two brothers together. It was obvious how much they loved each other. Still, it was hard to believe they'd only known each other for a little more than ten years.

"Declan called your doctor," Bram told Brier.

In the midst of stirring the gravy, Brier spun around, flinging the dark brown liquid onto the floor. "Really? What'd he say?"

"That he'd like to see you off your medication for at least ten days before he makes a final decision."

"Wait. What?" Jackie broke in.

Brier took the pan of gravy off the burner and grabbed a paper towel to wipe the floor. "I told Bram I wanted to get my driver's licence, but before I can, I need to go off my pills."

Jackie was surprised Bram would even consider it. He'd heard the story of Brier's meltdown at the Triple Spur after Jackie had left for the job in the Middle East.

"You think that's a good idea?" he asked Bram and Declan.

"According to my love-sick brother, you make him calm enough that he doesn't need the medicine anymore." Bram chuckled. "Though from what I heard when I walked into this house earlier, I'm beginning to question whether calm is the appropriate word."

Jackie could tell by Bram's expression he was trying to downplay his concerns about Brier coming off his pills. He decided to let the subject slide for the moment and get with Bram later. It wasn't that he didn't believe in Brier, but his lover's meltdowns in the past had proved detrimental to Brier's health. The last thing Jackie wanted was for Brier to hurt himself again.

* * * *

"Hello?" Jackie answered the phone.

"Hey, it's me. Just calling to check on Brier," Bram said.

"What? Isn't he there at work?" Jackie's heart sped up as he thought of all the things that could've gone wrong. Brier had been off his medication for eight days without any problems.

"Yeah, he's here. I can keep an eye on him here, it's what happens the rest of the day that I'm asking about," Bram told him.

"Oh." Jackie breathed a sigh of relief.

"He's good. He's found if he starts to feel anxious, pumping iron helps," Jackie continued.

"Just make sure he doesn't do too much of it. He became obsessed with lifting right after you left and we both know how that ended."

"Yeah. I'll watch him."

"Listen, the reason I called is because I received a message from the Oklahoma State Police."

Jackie's stomach dropped. "And?"

"The FBI arrested Rick earlier this morning in Lubbock, Texas."

"The FBI? Why are they in on this?" Jackie questioned.

"Because the state guys tracked a string of complaints involving Rick Sutcliff across four states. Seems our guy has been a busy pervert."

"So what does it mean for Brier?"

"Well that's what I'm trying to determine. The message said the FBI wanted to question Brier, but I'd already talked to the state guys and told them he wasn't up to it. From the message, I'd say the FBI doesn't give a fuck what Brier wants."

"Typical." Jackie rubbed the back of his neck.

"So what do we tell Brier?" Jackie asked.

"I don't know. I'm not sure he can even get through a simple questioning session without his medication. The first time he had to tell the police about those bastards molesting him while he was in the hospital, it really did a number on his emotional control."

"It'll break his heart if you put him back on it though. He's so damn proud of himself for working his anxieties out on his own. Besides, he's been studying the driver's manual every single evening." The whole thing made Jackie sick to his stomach. It was bad enough Rick and the other assholes took advantage of patients in a mental hospital, but to make those same patients go through the torture of telling and retelling their stories should be a crime in itself.

"I'll call Declan and we'll decide what's best."

Jackie felt he'd been slapped in the face. "Wait. You and Declan are gonna decide? Don't I have a say in this?"

Bram cleared his throat. "Sure you do, it's just that Brier's my legal responsibility."

And there was the crux of the matter. Despite loving and living with Brier, Jackie knew he had no legal say-so in the man's life. "That's something we need to talk about."

Bram sighed heavily into the phone. "Declan said this was going to become an issue. I'll tell you the same thing I told him. I know you care for my brother, and I thank God you do, but it's too early in your relationship to consider something so long-term."

"Fuck you," Jackie seethed. "How long were you with Declan before you knew you wanted him forever?"

"You can't compare the two, Jackie, and you know it," Bram sputtered.

"Why, you think because Brier isn't as intelligent as Declan that my love can't be real?"

"Stop putting words into my mouth," Bram yelled.

"And you stop spouting off and take a moment to determine how you really feel. In the meantime, I think we should tell Brier about Rick when we're together."

Bram started to say something, but Jackie cut him off. "Yeah, I know, you'll have to talk to Declan. Whatever. Just don't tell Brier without me being there."

Jackie hung up and slammed his fist against the kitchen table, upsetting his bowl of soup. "Fuck!"

* * * *

"We're gonna swing by and pick Declan up before I take you home," Bram told Brier.

Brier looked at his brother and shrugged. "Okay."

He didn't know what was going on, but Bram had acted strange all afternoon. Brier had gone into Bram's office earlier and found his twin arguing with Declan on the phone. When Bram had spotted Brier in the doorway, he whispered something into the receiver and hung up. Bram didn't say anything about the argument he'd had with Declan, but Brier could tell it was really bothering him.

"Are you taking Declan out to dinner?" he asked, trying to start a conversation.

"No," Bram replied.

When it was obvious he wasn't going to get any more out of Bram, Brier started to wring his hands. He hated that Bram wouldn't talk to him. Brier knew if he was like a normal brother, Bram would tell him everything.

"What's wrong?" Bram asked, gesturing to Brier's hands.

"Nothing," Brier mumbled.

"Bullshit. You're feeling anxious again, aren't you?" Bram accused.

"I can handle it."

Brier didn't miss the way Bram gripped the steering wheel tighter. "What? You think I can't?"

"Damn. I didn't say that. Why does everyone feel the need for a confrontation today?"

Brier jumped slightly in his seat. He wasn't used to Bram yelling at him, and Brier immediately felt bad for snapping at his brother in the first place. "Sorry, didn't mean to make you mad."

Bram pulled into the driveway in front of the house. Putting the car into park, he turned to Brier. "I'm sorry, too. I didn't mean to yell. It's just been a bad day."

Brier bit his lip. He didn't know if he should bring up the fight he knew Bram had had earlier with Declan. "Are you mad at Declan, too?"

"No," Bram soothed, reaching out to put his hand on Brier's thigh. "Sometimes couples have disagreements. That's all it was."

Brier nodded and opened the door when he spotted Declan coming out of the house. "I'll get in back."

"You don't have to, you know," Bram called after him.

Settling into the back seat, Brier grinned. "Yeah, I know, but I also know you want to kiss him when he gets in."

Bram was still chuckling when Declan sat in the front passenger seat. With a wink towards Brier, Bram pulled Declan in for a kiss.

"What was that for?" Declan asked when Bram released him.

"To put Brier's mind at ease. I don't think he likes it when we argue."

Declan reached across the back of the seat and gave Brier an affectionate pat on the knee. "Brier's not the only one."

Bram backed out of the drive and headed towards Jackie's house. "Mind if Declan and I come in for a few minutes?" Bram asked.

Brier knew it was pizza night, but he didn't want to be rude. "No, that's fine. But if you stay too long, you'll have to eat pizza with us. Jackie has to take his medicine with food and he needs it by six."

"Pizza night? Yum." Declan rubbed his stomach. "You're lucky. Bram never lets me order pizza."

Brier hugged himself, feeling special because Jackie loved him so much. "Jackie said there's no reason I should have to cook every night, so Wednesdays are pizza and Saturdays we order Chinese."

"Lucky dog," Declan laughed.

Brier thought of all the little things Jackie did for him. "Yeah, I am pretty lucky."

Chapter Four

Sitting on the sofa, Jackie rubbed more cream into the tender skin of his stump. He knew the new prosthetic would take some time to get used to, but it sure made for a sore couple of days. At least he was getting around with the aid of crutches, and although he was anxious to get back to work, he knew taking things slow would pay off in the end.

He heard the car pull up outside and quickly slid back into his modified jeans. The conversation he was about to have had set like a stone in his gut all afternoon. How Brier would react to the news the FBI had arrested Rick was anyone's guess.

The phone call with Bram earlier in the day still had his blood a tad hot. What the hell did he need to do to prove himself to the guy? Didn't Bram realise how special his brother was? The fantastic sex was only a small part of Brier's charm. The man had the biggest heart of anyone Jackie had met.

The front door opened and a smiling Brier walked in with Bram and Declan in tow. His lover shrugged out of his jacket on his way to Jackie's chair.

"Hey, don't you look happy," Jackie greeted, tilting his head up for a kiss.

"Of course I'm happy, I'm home with you."

Brier grinned and gave Jackie another kiss. "Do we have any of that grape Kool-Aid left?"

Seeing the opportunity to talk with Bram and Declan alone for a minute, Jackie shook his head. "Sorry, I had it for lunch. Would you mind making some more?"

"Nope. How 'bout cherry this time?"

"Sounds good, babe."

Brier turned to Declan and Bram who'd made themselves comfortable on the couch. "Can I bring you some?"

Bram chuckled. "No thanks. I'd rather have a beer if you have one."

"I'll take a glass," Declan spoke up.

With a nod and a jump in his step, Brier retreated to the kitchen. Jackie watched his lover until he was out of sight. Would he ever tire of that cute muscled ass?

"He seems to be in a pretty good mood," Jackie observed.

"Now," Bram replied. "It's one of the things that bothers me. On the way over he was anxious and out of sorts. Now he's Mr. Happy-Go-Lucky."

"Are you sure it wasn't you who was anxious and out of sorts? Or *maybe* it's possible that I'm actually good for him. I think it's obvious he's happy with me."

Bram leaned back on the couch and rubbed his hands over his face. "I never said you weren't good for him. I know what you mean to Brier."

"Then what is it?" Jackie prodded.

Bram sighed. "No matter how hard he works, in some respects, Brier will always be more like a child than a man. I know that you care for him, but no one can expect you to want that forever."

Anger filled his veins. Jackie wished he could launch himself across the room and plough his fist into Bram's face. He leant forward in the chair to give Bram a piece of his mind when he noticed Declan had gone pale. Following Declan's gaze, Jackie spotted Brier in the doorway, bottle of beer in hand.

Jackie's heart plummeted at the hurt expression on his lover's face. Without saying a word, Brier turned and retreated to the kitchen once again. Bram's indrawn breath signalled he'd also seen Brier.

"Fuck!" Jackie reached for his crutches to go after Brier, but was stopped by Bram.

"I'll go talk to him."

"No," Declan said, pushing Bram back to the sofa. "I think you've done enough for the moment. I'll go."

Jackie didn't miss the narrowing of Declan's eyes when he said it. Evidently this wasn't the first discussion the two of them had had regarding Brier. Jackie followed Declan with his eyes as the smaller man disappeared into the kitchen. He turned his attention back to Bram. "I think there are a few things we need to get straight."

* * * *

"Brier?" Declan called.

Brier squeezed his muscled frame further into the corner of the tool shed. His head was throbbing and his heart felt broken. He lifted his arm to wipe away the tears and knocked over a rake, sending several garden tools to the ground in a loud clanking of metal on metal. *Dammit.*

Brier closed his eyes, hoping Declan wouldn't see him. He heard the shed door open, the evening's pink sunlight filtering in against his closed lids.

"Brier?"

Brier felt the brush of Declan's body as his friend sat in the dirt beside him. A comforting arm wrapped itself around him, and Declan's head landed on Brier's shoulder. "I'm sorry."

Opening his eyes, Brier once again attempted to wipe away the ever-flowing tears. "I hate being me," he sobbed.

"No," Declan pulled Brier's head down to place a kiss on his forehead. "Don't ever feel that way."

Brier hiccupped and stared into Declan's sad face. He knew his friend loved him, but did Declan see him the way Bram did? Did Jackie see him that way?

"I try so hard," he gasped as another sob escaped him. "But people will never see me any different, no matter what I do."

Declan's cheeks became wet with his own tears. "That's not true. I love Bram with all my heart, but sometimes he says things..." Declan shook his head. "He feels guilty. Every time he looks at you, he's reminded that he couldn't protect either you or Thor against your father's abuse. I think by trying to protect you now, he's attempting to make up for that. Bram goes too far and it's something he's going to have to deal with, but don't ever let what another person says affect the way you see yourself."

When Brier attempted to look away, Declan caught his chin and held it. "How many times do I have to tell you what a special person you are for you to believe it? And if I'm not mistaken, Jackie sees you the same way."

"But Bram was right. Jackie deserves someone who's smart. He's really, really smart. He reads the newspaper and watches the news. Sometimes he'll start to say something about junk he's seen or read and then stops himself. I think he'd like to talk to me about stuff, but then he's afraid I won't understand."

The corner of Declan's mouth tilted up. "Perhaps Jackie needs a swift kick in the ass as well."

Brier shook his head. "No, I could never hurt Jackie."

Declan chuckled, and rubbed the top of Brier's head playfully. "I didn't mean you should really kick him. I just mean you should tell him that it hurts your feelings when he does that. He may not even be aware he's doing it."

A small bug on the ground caught Brier's attention. He reached down and picked the black beetle up, letting it crawl around his hand. "Do you agree with Bram? Do you think Jackie will get tired of living with a stupid person?"

"Now you listen up, Brier. You are not stupid," Declan began, tapping a finger on Brier's head. "What was damaged up here was not your fault. Give yourself some credit, will ya? Look at all the things you've accomplished since being released from the hospital. You have a full-time job, a savings account, and most importantly, you've found true love. I don't doubt for a second that Jackie will always love you. But it takes work, hard work. You have to learn to be honest with him. Tell him how you feel and when he makes you mad or upset, let him have it."

Brier returned his attention to the bug crawling up his arm. "I know I need to work on standing up for myself, but when I get mad, I can't always control it."

He set the beetle back on the ground. "I don't want people to be afraid of me."

"You're still going to counselling aren't you?" Declan asked.

"Yeah."

Declan stood and brushed the dirt from the seat of his pants. "Maybe you should take Bram with you sometime. You weren't the only one hurt by your father's actions."

Brier blinked several times. He'd never considered Bram might need to talk to Dr. Morgan. His brother always seemed so strong. "I should go in and say I'm sorry, huh?"

Declan held out his hand to help pull Brier to his feet. "That's the last thing you should do. Bram's the one who owes *you* an apology."

Brier grinned and gave Declan a big squishy hug. "I love you."

"Good, because I love you too. Now let's go get that Kool-Aid fixed. All this talking has made me thirsty."

Brier nodded and led the way out of the shed. When they entered the kitchen, Jackie was sitting at the table.

"It appears you have all the help you need. I'll just go find Bram," Declan excused himself.

Feeling embarrassed by his childish behaviour, Brier returned to the task of fixing the Kool-Aid. He carefully measured the sugar and poured it into a pitcher.

"Brier?"

"Yeah," he answered without turning around. Brier tore open the two packets of cherry flavoured powder and poured them on top of the sugar.

"Will you come over here and talk to me?" Jackie asked.

Brier thought about everything Declan had said and sighed. Turning to face Jackie, he realised his lover had done nothing wrong. "I'm okay. Bram hurt my feelings, but Declan made me feel better."

Jackie opened his arms. "I bet I can make you feel even better."

Brier knew Jackie's leg had been sore the last several days because of his new leg, so he repositioned one of the chairs to face his lover.

Jackie shook his head. "The day I can't handle you on my lap is the day I'll be ready for a retirement home."

Brier knew Jackie was only joking, but the thought of the two of them being together that long warmed him. "I found a bug," Brier blurted.

"Huh?"

"In the shed. There was a pretty beetle. Kinda looked green." He knew he was stalling, but Brier really wasn't interested in rehashing his earlier pain.

"Cool. Next time you should bring it in to show me."

"Really? I didn't know you liked bugs." Brier faced Jackie and straddled his lap, trying to put the majority of his weight on his boyfriend's good leg.

Jackie grinned. "To be honest, I don't think I ever paid much attention to them before, but you have a way of helping me look at everything through a fresh set of eyes."

Brier tried to work out what Jackie meant by that. He finally decided to take Declan's advice. "What do you mean?"

Instead of answering right away, Jackie pulled Brier in for a kiss. "It's like Kool-Aid. I suppose I probably drank it as a kid, but I'd forgotten how great it tastes until you came along to remind me. There are a lot of things like that. I'm not sure if it's because you were shut inside a hospital for so long or what, but the simplest things bring you pleasure. I wish everyone had that gift. I think the world would be a much happier place if we stopped to enjoy the everyday beauty around us."

Wow. Do I really do that? Brier could tell Jackie meant what he'd said, and it made him proud.

"You know how much I love you, right?" Jackie asked, running his hands in circles against Brier's back.

"Yeah, I know." Brier wondered whether or not he should bring up the stuff he'd talked about with Declan.

He thought about a show he'd seen on TV about dog training. The man said you have to scold your dog when he does something wrong, not before or after. Brier decided to follow that same advice. Jackie hadn't done anything recently, so he decided to wait until he did or said something to hurt his feelings.

"I have a confession to make," Jackie told Brier.

"Really? Like church?"

Jackie smiled. "Yeah, something like that. I had an argument with Bram earlier."

Brier was shocked. Jackie never got mad at people. "About what?"

"You. Sometimes I get upset because Bram makes decisions about you without talking to me about them first."

"And that makes you feel sad?"

"Yes," Jackie mumbled, not meeting Brier's gaze.

"Jackie? Don't be sad," Brier soothed, cupping his boyfriend's cheeks.

"I'm ashamed of myself because I just realised something. I get my feelings hurt because I'm jealous, not because Bram doesn't consult me."

Brier chuckled. "Why would you be jealous of Bram?"

Jackie shrugged. "Because I think you depend on him more than you do me. I want to be your number one." Jackie rolled his eyes. "I know, it's stupid, huh?"

"Yeah," Brier agreed. "It is pretty silly because you are number one."

"What? I am?" Jackie's expression was so cute Brier wanted to give him a hundred million kisses.

"Yeah, silly. I love my brother, but it's not like I'm *in* love with my brother. Geeze, that would be wrong."

Laughing, Jackie gave Brier one of those really good kisses with the tongue that Brier liked so much. Wanting more, Brier held Jackie's head still while he thrust his tongue into his boyfriend's mouth.

When they broke apart for air, Jackie jerked his head towards the door. "There's something Bram needs to talk to you about. I'd like to sit in there with you, but if you don't want me to, I'll understand."

Brier's tummy started to feel funny. It always did that when he got nervous. He could tell by the way Jackie said it, it was something really important. "I'd like you to sit by me."

"As long as you need me to."

* * * *

Once he helped Brier finish the Kool-Aid and grab another beer for Bram, Jackie settled uneasily into his chair. He was still pissed at Bram for the things he'd said earlier, but he also knew this wasn't the time. They had more important items to discuss.

Jackie accepted the glass of cherry flavoured sugar water and smiled. "Thanks, babe."

After taking several sips, he put his glass on the side table and waited for Brier to join him. His lover settled on the arm of the chair and wrapped his arm around Jackie's shoulders.

"You need to talk to me?" Brier asked Bram.

Bram sat up on the edge of the couch and rested his elbows on his knees. "I'm not sure how to say this without just coming out with it. I got a call from the police. The FBI apprehended Rick in Texas."

"Apprehended?" Brier asked, a questioning look in his eyes.

Jackie put a comforting hand on Brier's thigh. "He means they caught him."

"Oh." Brier sat for a moment. "Oh! That's good, right?"

"Yep. But the FBI wants to talk to you. Ya know, to ask a few questions," Jackie explained further.

"Okay. Are they like the people that helped Gabe at the Triple Spur?"

"Not the same men, but yeah, they're the good guys. Do you think you feel up to answering some questions?"

"Sure. I'll need to meet them if I'm going to tell the court all the bad things Rick did."

Bram rose from the sofa to kneel at Brier's feet. "No, buddy. You won't be testifying in court."

Brier's back went ramrod straight. "Yes I will. I made a deal."

Jackie glanced from Bram to Brier. "A deal? With who, the police?"

Brier rolled his eyes. "Noooo, with God."

Jackie took a deep breath. He now knew what Brier was referring to. Both Brier and Bram had told Jackie about the long hours Brier had put in at the church after he'd found out about Jackie's accident.

"You mean in exchange for my life," he surmised.

"Yeah. I promised I'd do everything I could to be a better man if he saved you."

Jackie put his hand to the back of Brier's neck to pull his lover down for a kiss. "Thanks, babe, but I think God would understand if you didn't testify at this hearing."

Brier shook his head. "God may understand, but I wouldn't be able to forgive myself."

Tilting his head to the side, Brier studied the three men in the room. "Would any of you testify?"

"This isn't about us," Bram cut in, reaching for Brier's hand. "We both know how upsetting it will be for you. Unless you want to go back on your medication, there's absolutely no way you'd be able to handle it emotionally."

Brier gripped Bram's hand. Although Jackie wasn't being addressed directly, it wasn't difficult to see the vehemence swimming in Brier's eyes when he spoke. "I don't want to go back on the medicine, it makes me feel different. Please, let me do this. How am I supposed to become a better man if I run away the first time things get bad?"

Bram broke away from Brier's gaze to glance over his shoulder at Declan. "What do you think?"

Jackie was surprised when Declan's eyes swung towards him. "I think we should discuss it with Jackie, since he'll be the one travelling to Oklahoma with Brier, don't you?"

Jackie held his breath as Declan and Bram continued to stare at each other for several moments. Eventually, Bram glanced at Jackie. "What do you think?"

No one would ever believe how much peace that simple question filled him with. All he'd wanted was to be consulted about Brier's care. "I think Brier's a grown man. If he thinks he's strong enough to give it a shot, I say we let him. We can take his medicine with us in case he needs it, but I've got faith in him."

Jackie looked at Brier. "I believe in you."

Chapter Five

Brier rolled a chicken breast in bread crumbs and put it on a cookie sheet. "So this'll really taste like fried chicken?"

"Near enough, and it's a heck of a lot safer than frying it in oil," Lilly answered.

Safer. Everyone was always trying to keep him safe. Although he appreciated that his loved ones cared so much, it also made him sad. He set another piece in the pan and glanced at Lilly. "Is this how you fry your chicken?"

The older woman's expression softened, "Sometimes."

"But not always," Brier finished for her.

Picking up the baking sheet, Lilly put the pan into the oven. "Let's have a visit while that cooks."

Brier nodded and washed his hands. He knew he could talk to Ms. Lilly. It was one of the reasons he'd called and invited himself over to her house. After getting his hands dried he settled at the kitchen table with his glass of sweet tea.

Lilly's hand covered his. Brier noticed how thin it was. His other hand began tracing the blue veins standing out in stark relief against the pale skin. When he'd first met Lilly, she'd been almost as brown as him, but now she was sick a lot, and needed to stay inside, instead of riding the horses she loved.

"Ugly, aren't they?" Lilly chuckled.

Ugly? "No. I think they're neat. They remind me of the worms we used to dig up to go fishing."

Lilly's chuckle turned into a laugh. "Just what every woman loves to hear."

Brier suddenly realised he probably shouldn't have said that. "Oh, no, I'm sorry. I didn't mean to make you feel bad."

Lilly patted his hand. "You didn't. I was teasing."

Emotions threatened to overwhelm him. It never mattered what he said or did around Ms. Lilly. She loved him no matter what, and he knew it. He'd often wondered how different his life would've been if… "I wish you were my mom."

Lilly's frail hand gripped his momentarily. "I wasn't a good mother to Nicco. Haven't you heard the story?"

He thought of Nicco and how much he doted on his mother. Brier couldn't imagine why Lilly would say such a thing. "I know how much Nicco loves you."

"Yes, now, but it wasn't always that way. When Nicco was very young, I ran off and left him with his father. Many years passed before I had the chance to become a real mother to him, and then he didn't really need me for that."

"People always need a mother," Brier corrected, seeing the sadness in Lilly's eyes.

Brier swallowed around the lump in his throat. He thought of the mother he never knew growing up. He'd suffered his head injury as a direct result of his father's abusive anger, and had been given away to the state when his parents didn't feel like dealing with a stupid son.

It was many years before he'd grown into a man and was able to track his mother down after escaping from the mental hospital. For over thirty-five years all he'd thought about was finding his mom. He'd wanted her to throw open her arms and hug him. How many years had he hoped it had all been a mistake, and his mom still loved and wanted him? His head had been full of dreams but when he finally found his mom, she said really ugly things to him.

"I killed my mom," he admitted.

He still hadn't come to terms with what he'd done in a state of confusion, sadness and rage. He'd been lucky the judge agreed to send him back to the mental hospital instead of prison. Despite the years of intensive therapy, Brier knew it was the love and support of his brothers that helped him overcome his handicap.

Although he tried to be the man he wanted to be, nothing could erase the horrible things he'd done in his past. How could someone like Jackie really love him knowing what he'd done?

"I know," Lilly whispered.

"You do?" Brier shook his head. "And you still trust me to spend time with you?"

Tears slowly dripped down Lilly's face. "Of course I trust you. I love you like a son. I have since the first day Bram brought you over."

"Why? I've done really bad things."

"Yes, you have, but you were sick then. You're better now."

"Am I? Then why can't I make real fried chicken? Or talk to those FBI guys by myself? That's what I want, ya know. I don't want Jackie or Bram in there with me when I tell them."

"Tell them what? What're you afraid of them hearing?" Lilly asked.

Brier pulled his hands away from Ms. Lilly and put them into his lap. Gazing down at the table, he closed his eyes. "That I didn't say no to those men who hurt me."

He heard Lilly sigh and then a chair scooting out. When frail arms enveloped him, he was shocked. Brier looked up into the loving eyes of the older woman.

"Whether you said no or not isn't in question. The fact is, those men took advantage of their positions by having sex with you."

"But even though it hurt, sometimes I liked it when they would put their arms around me and hold me tight. What if the FBI guys decide I should go to jail, too? What if Jackie decides he doesn't love me anymore?"

Lilly squeezed him harder. "Have you talked to Jackie about what you're afraid of?"

"No!" he exclaimed, shaking his head.

Lilly kissed the top of Brier's head. He loved it when she did stuff like that. It made him feel safe. "You won't tell him, will ya?"

"No, it's not my place, it's yours. But I can tell you a thing or two. Regardless of what you felt when those men had sex with you, they did something wrong. You were a patient, and they should've respected that boundary."

Lilly knelt on the floor and gazed up at Brier. "Everyone has the desire to be held and loved. At the time you didn't know the difference. No one can fault you for that. Look into your heart. Now that you're loved by a good man, can you tell the difference between what those awful men did to you and how Jackie makes you feel?"

Making love with Jackie was nothing like what Rick and the other two had done to him. "Yeah."

Lilly smiled. "Then there's your answer. And don't sell Jackie short. I'm sure he'd understand everything you've just told me. Love like his doesn't go away, you just have to trust that."

Brier nodded. Deciding he'd had enough of being sad, he grinned. "So does that mean I can talk you into teaching me how to make real fried chicken?"

* * * *

Turning off the alarm, Jackie rolled back over and wrapped a still-sleeping Brier in his arms. They'd talked long into the night, and the emotions still showed in the puffiness surrounding his lover's eyes.

Their talk had been a hard one, but Jackie was glad they'd had it. He had no idea that Brier was worried about going to jail along with Rick, Jimmy and possibly Carl. Jackie just hoped he'd done a good job of reassuring his partner that going to jail wasn't an option, and he'd never stop loving him. That more than anything seemed to bring comfort to Brier.

"Hey, sleepyhead, it's time to get ready for work."

Brier grunted and snuggled in closer.

Jackie ran his hands across the soft skin of Brier's naked hip to land on one firm globe of his lover's ass. "I'm picking you up at three to take you to get your driver's licence."

Brier's eyes popped open. "Really? I didn't study last night."

Jackie chuckled, slipping his finger between Brier's butt cheeks to trace the still loose hole. They'd made love several times the previous night and Brier's body, it seemed, was ready for another round. The last time they'd come together, they'd fallen asleep with Jackie still buried to the hilt in Brier's body. The faint traces of his seed under his finger allowed him to push in easily.

Brier moaned and crawled his way up Jackie's body until their lips met in a deep morning kiss. Brier was the only man Jackie had ever been with who actually tasted good in the morning. Too bad he couldn't say the same for himself, but Brier never seemed to mind.

Swinging his leg over, Brier straddled Jackie's lap. "Want you," he whispered, breaking the kiss.

Always willing to make his lover feel good, Jackie reached for the lube on the side table. Handing it to Brier, he grinned. "Slick me up, babe."

Jackie chuckled as Brier licked his lips.

"Taste first," Jackie replied.

Jackie removed his finger from the gorgeous man's ass, allowing Brier to scoot down and envelop his hard shaft in that hot mouth he was so in love with. As Brier's tongue pressed against the large vein on the underside of Jackie's cock he couldn't help but to moan. "Feels so good, too good. If you keep it up you'll get breakfast instead of the fucking you're after."

Laughing, Brier pulled his mouth from Jackie's cock and picked up the lube. "As much as I like breakfast, I like you inside me even more."

The cold lube dripping down his cock was in stark contrast to the warm mouth of a few seconds earlier and Jackie's cock jumped in surprise.

The action made Brier laugh harder. "I like it when it dances for me."

"It'll always dance for you," Jackie answered.

Brier used the rest of the lube on his fingers to slick his own hole before shimmying back up Jackie's body. He lined Jackie's cock up with his hole and sat back, impaling himself in one smooth move.

"Damn, babe," Jackie groaned, feeling the squeeze of Brier's muscles around his shaft.

He reached out and pulled Brier in for a kiss, thrusting his tongue deep into Brier's mouth as he pumped his cock into his lover's ass. Aware of the time, he rolled them both over until Brier was under him.

His stump was healed enough to hold his weight, as he positioned his cock at Brier's hole once more. Gripping Brier's ankles in his hands, Jackie spread his lover's legs wide as he drove in and out of the tight sheath. He felt his balls draw up and gave Brier a warning. "Can't hold back any longer."

Brier nodded and jacked his own erection faster. Gazing down into those dark brown eyes, Jackie slipped over the edge into pure bliss. His climax was so intense he collapsed even before his cock was finished spurting its bounty.

It wasn't until after he'd regained his senses that Jackie realised Brier had already come as well. Dammit, he'd missed it. Few things gave him greater pleasure than watching Brier's face when he came.

He nuzzled his face against Brier's sweaty neck. "I love you."

Brier sighed. "I love you too."

Jackie groaned when Brier pushed against his chest. "I need to get into the shower or I'm going to be really late for work."

Jackie moved, his cock slipping from Brier's ass. "I know. I'll get dressed while you take a shower."

Brier swung his legs over the side of the bed and stood. "What about you? Aren't you gonna take one?"

"Later, after I take you to work. If I jump in with you, we'll never get you there on time."

Brier turned and strutted towards the bathroom, doing his best to tempt Jackie into joining him. As much as Jackie would've enjoyed running soapy hands all over Brier's gorgeous body, he knew how much getting to work on time meant to his partner.

Jackie was determined to make the day a good one for Brier. He'd already planned to take his lover to get his licence, but what Brier didn't know was about the small dinner party he'd planned for afterward.

With the FBI interview scheduled for the following day, Jackie felt it was important to surround Brier with the people he cared about. Hopefully, the added support would help calm his lover's nerves.

He heard the shower turn off, snapping him out of his thoughts. Reaching for his prosthesis, Jackie put his thoughts on the back burner.

* * * *

"I still can't believe you got a perfect score on both the written and driving portions of the test," Jackie proclaimed, shaking his head. "You're so amazing. I actually took that damn thing twice before I passed."

Brier was filled with pride at Jackie's statement. He knew it had helped that the woman giving him the test had thought he was cute. She even flirted with him. Brier still didn't know what to make of that. He thought of the small piece of paper in his pocket. "Did you see that lady give me her phone number?"

"What? Who?" Jackie asked.

"That nice lady who gave me the test. She gave me her number and asked me to call her."

Jackie whistled. "Damn, babe, she was a good-looker, too. Did you say anything?"

"Umm, no, not really. I just told her that I didn't think my boyfriend would like it, but she told me to keep it and ask you about a threesome." Brier glanced over at Jackie. "What did she mean by that?"

Jackie chuckled. "She meant she'd be interested in fucking us both at the same time."

"Oh. Oooh, yuck. I don't think I could have sex with a woman. I don't know anything about their parts, but I've heard they're different from mine."

Laughing, Jackie gestured towards a Mexican restaurant. "Pull in there and let's get something to eat."

Brier did as instructed. When he turned off the engine, Jackie pulled him into his arms and kissed him. "You know, if you'd like to try sex with a woman, I wouldn't stop you. I wouldn't like it, and I'd be jealous as hell, but I'd understand."

That shocked Brier. "Have you ever done it?"

"Sure. When I was younger, I fucked quite a few women before I realised it wasn't the woman, but their womanly parts that I didn't get off on."

Brier reached between them and massaged Jackie's cock through his jeans. "What do they feel like?"

"Soft and squishy. Some women have big boobs, too large to fit in your hand, while others have itty bitty breasts that kinda look like a man's only squishy instead of hard with muscle."

Brier managed to unzip Jackie's jeans as he talked. Fishing out the semi-hard cock, he licked his lips. "They don't have this though, do they?"

Jackie spread his thighs further apart and shook his head. "Nope. They have two warm holes to fuck instead of just the one that we have."

Brier thought about it. It all sounded so alien to him. "I can't imagine what that would look like, but I'm pretty sure I'd prefer this anyway."

He continued to stroke Jackie's cock, making sure to watch for people walking close to the car. Although he was curious about women, he really couldn't imagine enjoying sex with anyone besides Jackie, but that didn't mean his lover would always be satisfied without a woman. "Do you want to? Have sex with that woman, I mean?"

Jackie carefully removed Brier's hand from around his cock. "No, babe. I've had my fill of pussy. I much prefer what you have hanging between your legs, but now isn't the time. We've got reservations inside for dinner."

Brier felt let down when Jackie tucked his cock back into his underwear and zipped up. "Later? Cuz I'm really hard now."

Chuckling, Jackie kissed him, slow and deep. "Just try and keep me away from this pretty ass."

Feeling much better about the rebuff, Brier climbed out the driver's side. Although it took his boyfriend longer to get the single crutch he was down to and get out of the car, Brier knew from experience Jackie preferred to do it himself. He noticed Jackie staring at the front of his jeans and grinned. Yeah, he was still as hard as a rock and nothing would make him soft until he came, it was just the way his body worked.

Before going inside, Jackie casually brushed the front of Brier's jeans. "Am I going to be tempted by this throughout dinner?"

"I sure hope so," Brier quipped.

Brier held the door for Jackie, not ashamed in the least to be sporting a woody that tested the zipper in his denims. It was a natural state when around his boyfriend and others would have to get used to it.

He was concentrating so hard on getting Jackie in bed, the appearance of his brother, and the rest of his friends, surprised him. The first thing out of Bram's mouth shocked him even more.

"So, let me see it, brother," Bram demanded, arms crossed over his chest.

Brier thought his eyes would bug out of his head. He glanced worriedly at Jackie. "What? Here?"

"Of course here. Jackie said you passed your test. I want to see your licence picture. It has to be better than mine."

With a sigh of relief, and a red face, Brier dug the wallet out of his back pocket. He'd never admit out loud what he thought his brother was asking to see. He handed over the small plastic card with pride. "The lady said I got an A."

Jackie ran a hand down Brier's spine. "Although from the sounds of it, the woman was after more than giving him the test."

Bram's brows shot up. "Well, well, aren't you just the ladies man."

Brier rolled his eyes and took his licence back. "Stop teasing me."

He found two chairs at the table and pulled one out for Jackie. "Hi, everybody."

It was nice to see Ms. Lilly, Nicco, Amir and Mac. He sat down amongst a round of congratulations. Brier noticed Jackie's best friend was missing from the group. "Where's Taggert?"

Jackie rested his crutch against the wall behind him and put his hand on Brier's thigh. "He's at the safe-house with Lon and Alec."

Brier leant over and whispered in Jackie's ear. "Is all this for me?"

Jackie turned his head and gave Brier a brief but passionate kiss. "Of course it's for you, or do you know someone else who passed his driving test today with flying colours?"

Brier stared into his lover's eyes. Jackie was always so thoughtful when it came to things like that. "Thanks."

Jackie gave Brier's leg a squeeze before sliding his hand up and down the inside of Brier's thigh. "Thank me later."

"Oh, I intend to. Several times," he added.

* * * *

After seeing the two FBI agents out, Jackie sat next to a shaken Brier. "You okay?"

Brier nodded, but continued to study his hands, which had become almost raw from the constant rubbing his lover did when he was anxious. "They made it sound like Rick was really a bad man."

"They just told the truth, babe. Rick's been skirting the authorities for years. Most of his victims aren't as brave as you."

He wrapped a comforting arm around his partner. "Do you still think you want to testify?"

Brier's back stiffened. "Sure I do."

Jackie closed his eyes and rested his chin against the top of Brier's head. According to the agents who'd just left, they'd been close to pinning charges on Rick once before, but the victim had backed out before it could go to trial. Even though they hadn't come out and said it, Jackie got the feeling they believed the victim had been threatened in some way.

Normally it wouldn't have scared Jackie, but he still wasn't able to walk like he used to. He questioned whether or not he'd be able to protect Brier if it ever came to it. Jackie knew he needed to talk to Mac, but it would have to wait. "Are you hungry?"

"No." Brier didn't say anything else for a few minutes. "Would you just watch some TV and hold me like this for a while?"

Jackie could tell by the slight catch in Brier's speech that his lover was struggling to hold himself together. Without taking the medication, he was doing remarkably well considering the circumstances.

"Would you rather watch the tube in the bedroom? That way you can sleep if you want."

Brier shook his head again, burying his face against Jackie's chest. "I don't want to move from here."

Jackie reached over to the side table and grabbed the remote. He got himself into a comfortable position with his foot up on the coffee table and turned on a baseball game. He knew from experience the white noise of the cheering crowd always put Brier to sleep.

His lover spread his legs out on the couch and rested his head on a pillow in Jackie's lap. Jackie couldn't keep his fingers from running through the silky black strands as he began going over all the things that needed to be done before they left for Oklahoma.

Within minutes, Brier's breathing evened out as he drifted off to sleep. Jackie ran a finger down the bronzed skin of his lover's cheek. Part of him felt guilty at the bargain Brier had made with God, but the other part felt nothing but pride. The fact that Brier was willing to hold up his end of the promise spoke volumes about his lover's character. Jackie wondered how many others would keep their word given the same circumstances.

Chapter Six

"How's the new job going?" Mac asked, taking a seat in front of Jackie's desk.

"Fine so far." Jackie twirled a pen between his fingers. The phone call he'd received from Bram earlier was weighing heavily on his mind. "You talk to Bram?"

"Yeah," Mac confessed.

"I just don't get it. Why isn't Brier's testimony enough to convict those assholes?"

Jackie dropped the pen and rubbed his eyes. "Brier's going to feel like he reneged on his deal with God."

Mac shook his head. Everyone at Three Partner's knew what that promise meant to Brier. "There might be a way to still put Rick before a judge, but I'm not sure about the other two."

"I'm listening." Jackie leaned against the top of his desk. He wasn't as concerned with the other two. According to Brier, Rick had pretty much made them do it so they couldn't tell on him for fucking the patients.

"There has to be more people this happened to. What if we talk to the federal prosecutor and see if he won't get us a list..."

"And we could talk them into joining Brier," Jackie finished for his friend.

"Exactly."

Jackie wondered if he should mention any of it to Brier before they talked to the prosecutor. Although Brier had been on edge several times since going off his medication, he'd done a damn good job of coping. Would the news that Rick could walk away push his lover over the edge?

Mac cleared his throat. "I think Bram needs to be the one to call the prosecutor. I know it's been a sore subject between the two of you, but he's still Brier's legal guardian. I think the prosecutor would take that into account when trying to build a stronger case against Rick."

Jackie ground his teeth. It was still an area of his relationship with Brier that he didn't like to think about. When would Bram see his love for Brier was the real deal?

He finally nodded. "Would you talk to him about it? It's still a pretty hot topic between the two of us."

"Sure." Mac sat for a second before continuing. "You know he loves Brier with all his heart, right?"

Jackie couldn't sit still any longer. He rose from his chair and began pacing the small office, glad to finally be free of the cane. Although he still had a small limp, the therapists assured him his walking would only get better.

"I'm torn in that respect. Yeah, I know Bram only wants what's best for Brier, but it hurts to know he doesn't think what's best for his brother is me."

Mac rose and put a hand to Jackie's shoulder. "I don't think that has anything to do with it. Everyone with eyes can see how much you and Brier mean to each other. You've been damn good for him. He's grown more with you than he has since he was released from the hospital. I think that may be part of Bram's problem."

"How the fuck does that make any sense? What? Bram doesn't want Brier to get better?"

Gripping both of Jackie's shoulders, Mac looked him directly in the eyes. "You weren't around when Bram first found out Brier even existed. I've known Bram for years and have never seen him that upset. I don't pretend to understand it, but Bram feels incredibly guilty. Taking care of Brier is the only way he knows how to atone for that guilt. When Brier was finally released from the hospital, Bram picked up his entire life and moved here so Brier could be with him and Declan."

"I know that, but why can't he see how much better Brier's getting? Hell, I'm not sure he needs a guardian at all anymore."

"That's because you weren't here when Brier had his meltdown after you left."

Mac sighed and released his hold on Jackie. "Look, I love Brier as if he were my own brother, but he's not only socially stunted, he's mentally handicapped. I don't know the extent of brain damage he suffered as an infant, but Brier's inability to control his temper is still a real issue."

Jackie thought of the things he'd helped Brier work through in the past several weeks. "I'm good for him."

"Yeah, you are. I don't think anyone is disputing that. Bram's just worried that dealing with Brier's limitations might become too much. It's a valid worry."

Jackie crossed his arms. "Amir puts himself into some pretty dangerous situations. What would happen...?"

"Stop right there," Mac ordered.

"You see my point though, right? I know you, Mac. You wouldn't love that man any less if he wasn't perfect."

Mac scoffed. "He's far from perfect now, but I see your point."

Why was it so hard for people to understand how much he loved Brier? He felt like he could talk until he was blue in the face and still be questioned. "Believe me, I'm not trying to take Bram's brother away from him. I just don't like the idea of him always making the decisions for Brier. Because what affects Brier, affects me."

Mac nodded. "I get ya. I'll talk to Bram about calling the prosecutor. Maybe while I'm at it, I'll bring up a few of the things we've discussed."

Jackie held out his hand. One of the reasons Mac made such a good boss and friend was his ability to see both sides of a situation. "I'd appreciate anything you could do."

After Mac left, Jackie called the accounting office. "Hey, Sheila, you got a good-looking stud wandering around your office with an empty stomach?"

* * * *

After picking up a couple of sub sandwiches, Jackie suggested they go to the park. Brier liked the idea of being spread out on a blanket in the sun with the man he loved, so he readily agreed.

He let Jackie drive because he knew his lover needed the practice more than he did. Brier hated to toot his own horn, but he had passed his driver's test with flying colours.

Glancing over at his boyfriend, Brier's brow furrowed. Jackie had such a look of concentration on his face it began to worry him. "Everything okay?"

Jackie didn't even acknowledge that Brier had spoken. Biting his lip, Brier reached over and put a hand to his lover's leg. "Jackie?"

"Huh?" Jackie asked.

"What's wrong?"

Jackie turned to gaze at Brier, his eyes full of worry. "Nothing's wrong."

Jackie pulled into the park and stopped beside one of the shelter houses. Brier wasn't sure what to do. He remembered his talk with Declan. "Why do you do that to me?"

Switching off the engine, Jackie turned to Brier. "Do what, baby?"

"Keep things from me. Sometimes…it hurts my feelings." He knew it was because Jackie didn't think he was smart enough to understand bad things, but Brier knew he understood more than people gave him credit for.

Jackie opened his mouth to say something before snapping it shut. He got out of the car and slammed the door. Brier sat there, his insides making him feel like he might throw up. He watched as Jackie paced back and forth in front of the car. By the way Jackie's lips were moving, Brier had a feeling he was fighting with himself over something. Brier just hoped it wasn't him. He wasn't sure what he'd do if Jackie left him.

After several minutes, Jackie walked back to the car and opened Brier's door. Without a word, Jackie held his hand out. With a deep breath, Brier took it and Jackie helped him out of the car.

With Brier trapped between Jackie's broad chest and the car, he waited. It wasn't long before Jackie leaned in and kissed him. Brier was so relieved, he opened immediately, accepting his lover's tongue. His arms went around Jackie's neck as he sank heart and soul into his boyfriend's embrace.

Before things had a chance to go further, Jackie broke the kiss. "I'm sorry if I do that to you."

Brier's mind was so foggy from the kiss he didn't know what Jackie was talking about. "Do what?"

"Keep things from you. There's no excuse for it. It's wrong and it's as simple as that." Jackie bent his head down and wiped the sweat from his forehead on his biceps.

"Okay, so will you tell me what's wrong?" Brier asked.

"Bram got a call from the prosecutor. He doesn't have enough evidence to make a conviction in your case on any of the three men."

"Not even Rick?"

Jackie shook his head. "In all the time Rick's been doing this, there have only been two people who've filed charges. Both of whom were somehow scared off before a trial could even be set."

Jackie stepped back and motioned towards a picnic table. "Let's talk while we eat our lunch."

Brier turned and grabbed the sack of sandwiches from the floorboard and handed them to Jackie before pulling their large sweet teas out of the cup holders. He followed Jackie to the table and sat down.

Once he began eating his sandwich, Brier let his mind travel back over what Jackie had told him. How was it possible that Rick and the other men could go free?

"Is it because they think I'm too stupid to know what happened?"

Jackie set his cup down and reached across the table to grip Brier's hand. "You're not stupid. You can't think of yourself like that."

Brier nodded. "But is that the reason?"

He watched as a muscle in Jackie's jaw began to move. "There's no physical proof of what they did. All the prosecutor has to go on is your word. Since you're the only one who's had the guts to come forward, he's afraid to spend the government's money on a trial."

Brier ran his fingers through his hair. "Doesn't the government take money out of my cheque every week?"

"Yeah."

"So isn't the government's money also my money?"

Jackie grinned. "Yeah."

Brier chewed his bottom lip. "Well maybe I just don't understand things, but shouldn't they ask me if I still want to try and get him sent to jail?"

Jackie stood and leaned over the table. Putting his hands on either side of Brier's head he pulled him in for a kiss. "Yes."

Sitting back down, Jackie laughed. "There's nothing about you that's stupid, babe. Let's get back to the office and give the prosecutor a call back. Maybe we can convince him to talk to Jared and Peter."

* * * *

Jackie hung up the phone and turned to Brier. The hopeful expression was now gone from Brier's face. Although the prosecutor had been very receptive earlier in the day, the phone call he'd just received had dashed their hopes. Jackie didn't tell Brier, but the FBI had had no choice but to let Rick go. Jackie wondered what it would mean to any hopes of furthering their case against the slimeball. "He said neither Jared, nor Peter will talk about what happened. I'm sorry, babe, it doesn't look good."

Brier shook his head. "Well maybe we could try calling them."

With an internal sigh of exasperation, Jackie held out his arms. "Come here."

Brier crawled into Jackie's lap. Despite the situation they were in, Jackie's cock took notice of the wiggling ass of his lover. He tried to reign in his lust enough to explain things to his partner, but Brier's soft sweatpants weren't making it easy.

"We can't make someone talk to us if they don't want to, babe. Maybe if we wait a few days we can try again."

Brier started playing with the buttons on Jackie's dress shirt, slowly slipping them through the hole one by one. "Why can't we go see them? I know if I talked to them they'd understand why telling the judge about Rick is the right thing to do."

Jackie allowed Brier to push the shirt from his shoulders. Maybe if he could distract Brier with sex he'd forget about Jared and Peter for the night. With a hand to the back of Brier's head, Jackie brought his lover's mouth to his left nipple.

Brier was eager to please and soon began licking and sucking the pebbled nub. Jackie's head fell against the back of the couch as he gave himself over to Brier's skilled mouth. Licking across Jackie's chest, his lover spent several moments teasing the other nipple before travelling south.

"You didn't answer my question," Brier reminded, unfastening Jackie's dress pants.

How the hell was he supposed to think with Brier mouthing his erection through his underwear? "What?"

Brier hooked his fingers under the elastic waistband and gave a tug. Jackie lifted his ass and Brier pulled the garments down his legs, over the prosthesis and off. Moving back between Jackie's spread thighs Brier poised his mouth over the leaking crown.

"I want to go see Jared and Peter."

Jackie thrust up trying to get his cockhead into Brier's mouth, but Brier was too quick and pulled back. *Shit.*

"We can't do that. If we push these guys too hard by showing up on their doorstep they could file a harassment complaint against us, and then we'd be the ones in trouble with the police."

"So you could get into trouble?" Brier asked.

"Yeah, we both could."

Brier's tongue absently licked the head of Jackie's cock. Jackie could tell his lover was deep in thought trying to work through what he'd been told. Jackie tried thrusting his hips towards Brier's mouth once again.

Brier glanced up, teasing his tongue along Jackie's shaft. "I don't want you to get into trouble."

"Good, now can we do this thing before my nuts turn blue?"

Chapter Seven

Brier made sure no one else was in Sebastian's office before he knocked on the open door. "Seb? Do you have a minute?"

Dressed in his customary low-rise jeans, black T-shirt and black leather blazer, Seb glanced over his shoulder. "Sure. Just give me a second while I find this elusive summary report."

Brier took a seat in front of the desk and crossed his right leg over his left knee. He'd always thought Seb was handsome in a dangerous sort of way. With long black hair and a neatly trimmed beard and moustache, Seb was the office bad boy.

"Finally!" Seb declared, holding up a thin file. He walked back to his chair and sat down. "Now, what can I do for ya?"

With shaking hands, Brier dug the small sheet of paper out of his back pocket. He handed it to Seb and smiled. He knew what he was about to do was wrong, but he didn't have much choice. The last thing he wanted was to get Jackie in trouble with the police, but he had to talk to Jared and Peter.

"I want to find a couple of my friends from the hospital, but I don't know where they're living now."

Seb looked at the names written on the sheet. "You want me to find them, is that it?"

"Yeah."

Seb leaned back in his chair and threaded his fingers together over his broad chest. "Why not ask Bram or Jackie?"

Brier quickly said another prayer, asking forgiveness before he told yet another lie. "They don't think I should be friends with Peter and Jared anymore. But I miss them. I thought I'd send them a letter, maybe we could be like pen-pals or something."

Reaching up, Seb ran his fingers through his short beard. "If anyone finds out, you can't tell them I did this."

"I won't. I promise." Brier used his index finger to cross his heart.

Looking at the slip of paper again, Seb picked up a pen. "What was the name of the hospital again?"

Brier smiled. The first part of his plan to keep his bargain with God had gone smoothly.

* * * *

Brier was doing the daily filing when he spotted Seb enter the room. He glanced over at Sheila who was staring intently at her computer screen. Seb stepped up and slid a folded piece of paper under the stack of files.

"Thanks," Brier whispered.

"Don't mention it. Ever," Seb answered, leaving the room.

Just in case Sheila had witnessed the exchange, he put several more files in their place before sliding the folded yellow sheet out and opening it. Jared was the closest, living in Lubbock, Texas. Peter was further away in Tulsa, but Brier knew he'd make the trip if he needed to.

Brier had vowed on his knees to step up and be the man Jackie deserved and he took that oath very seriously. Slipping the paper back under the files, he wondered if he was doing the right thing. He remembered the conversation he'd had with Jackie the previous night. No matter what, he knew he couldn't let his lover get into trouble with the police.

He thrummed his fingers on top of the metal file cabinet as he tried to figure out how he was going to borrow a car. If he took Jackie's, the police might think he was part of Brier's plan. No, he couldn't do that.

A hand to his shoulder spooked him and Brier let out a squeal as he jumped.

"Hey, hey, babe, it's just me."

Brier spun around to face Jackie. He wondered if his boyfriend could see the guilt of his earlier actions. "Hi. You scared me."

Chuckling, Jackie leaned in and placed a kiss on Brier's temple. "I didn't mean to. I thought you might be ready to go home."

Brier glanced at the stack of files yet to be put away. The yellow piece of paper was just sitting there out in the open. "Can you give me another fifteen minutes? I don't like to leave until everything is done."

"Would you like some help?" Jackie asked, reaching towards the stack.

"No!" Brier quickly stepped between Jackie and the file cabinet. "It's my job."

Jackie held up both hands and took a step back. "Okay. I'll go find something else to do."

Brier huffed. He knew Jackie had been trying to help, and now he'd made him mad. "I'm sorry. Please don't be mad at me."

Jackie took Brier in his arms and kissed him. "I'm not mad. You do what you need to and then come find me."

Seeing his chance, Brier cleared his throat. "Well, you could always go ask Bram if he'd let me use my savings to buy a car. I don't need anything fancy, but on days like this it would be nice for us to have two cars."

Jackie shook his head. "I don't mind waiting."

Brier fingered the light blue button of Jackie's work shirt. "Yeah, but I kinda wanted to stop by the church, too. See? It would be nice if I could make my own decisions about when I wanted to go home."

Jackie's body stiffened and he dropped his arms to his sides. "I'll go talk to Bram."

"Thanks."

Brier watched Jackie leave the room with mixed emotions. He wasn't sure what he'd said, but it was easy enough to tell his boyfriend wasn't very happy. Maybe he shouldn't have brought up the church.

Turning back to the file cabinet, he stuffed the paper with the addresses into his pocket. If he could buy a car then he wouldn't have to worry about stealing Jackie's, because he knew that's what it would be. Bram had taught him that to take something that wasn't yours was stealing, and the last thing Brier wanted was to go to jail.

* * * *

Bram was on the phone when Jackie stepped into his office. He could tell by the jovial conversation it had to be one of his buddies.

"Okay, tell Locky I'll get some more in the mail Saturday. Give everyone my love. Yeah, I will. Bye." Bram hung up the phone smiling. "That was Cree."

"Something up?" Jackie asked.

"Nope, Locky wanted to call to thank me for the books I'd taken him a few months back and to let me know he was all finished." Bram chuckled. "That part of the conversation was intercepted by Cree who wasn't happy his son was asking for more books in his own subtle way."

"Gotta love a kid who reads though."

"Yep, which is why I'll never listen to Cree when he tells me the boy has enough." Bram swung his legs onto the desk and leant back in his chair. "What's up?"

Following Bram's lead, Jackie made himself comfortable. "Is there something going on with Brier that I don't know about?"

Bram's black brows shot up. "No, not that I know of, why?"

"He wants a car of his own." Jackie shifted in his chair. He didn't like the implications of Brier's statement earlier. Was his lover trying to tell him something?

"Well, he's been saving his money for one. I guess I can't think of a reason he shouldn't be able to get one," Bram answered.

Jackie felt like a stone had landed in his gut. Just a few days earlier Bram was wrapping his brother in cotton wool, and now he up and agrees with Brier getting a car? It didn't make sense to Jackie. "Why the sudden change of heart?"

Bram grinned. "Declan helped me see a few things."

"Like?"

"Like if I didn't lighten up, I'd lose my brother entirely. I'd do just about anything to protect him, but Declan made me see I couldn't live his life for him."

"He said he wants to have the freedom to come home when he's ready." Jackie shrugged. Now he was sounding like the overprotective one. "I'm not sure what that means other than he doesn't want to be tied to me anymore."

Bram seemed to study Jackie for several moments. "I don't think you need to worry. Sounds like Brier's simply trying to exert his independence. Don't forget he's spent a lifetime doing what other people told him to do. Maybe he wants to feel he has more control over his own life now."

Why does that bother me so much? "So you think I should give him more space?"

"For a while, maybe. I think it's the same phase most of us went through in our teenage years. He loves you, but he also wants to prove to himself that he's man enough to do things on his own."

Jackie rested his head against the back of the chair. He shouldn't feel like he was being left behind, but he did.

The broader Brier's world became, the less chance he'd want to stick with him for the long haul. How many lovers had come and gone from his life over the years? He thought things would be different this time. He liked taking care of Brier. It made him feel safe knowing Brier needed him as much as he needed Brier. If his lover started gaining more independence, what use would he have for Jackie?

"You want to take him, or do you want me to?" Bram asked.

"Huh?" he asked, trying to get back into the conversation.

"To get a car?"

Jackie's head was pounding. He pinched the bridge of his nose, trying to clear his head. "I'll take him. Maybe we'll drive by one of the lots on the way home. Do you have a preference about what he should look at?"

Bram shook his head. "He's got a pretty big nest egg built up, so anything reasonably priced would be fine."

Jackie tapped his fingers against the arm of the chair. He didn't have anything else to say to Bram, but didn't quite know what to do with himself while he waited. Standing, he made sure to regain his balance on the artificial foot before turning towards the door.

"I guess I'll see how he's doing with the filing and give him the good news." Jackie just wished he felt better about it. He waved goodbye to Bram and started out the door, almost getting rundown by Brier in the process.

Jackie's knee hyper extended as he felt something give. Falling backward, Jackie was saved from a potentially embarrassing situation when Brier's arms wrapped around his waist.

"I'm so sorry," Brier apologised.

Steadying himself with his hands on Brier's shoulders, Jackie shrugged off the incident, swallowing the bile threatening to rise in his throat. "Don't worry. I'm fine."

He didn't dare tell Brier the movement had caused his artificial limb to dig into his tender flesh. "I think I'll go to the restroom before we leave."

Brier nodded and released his hold on Jackie. Trying his best to put one foot in front of the other, Jackie waited until he was out of sight before bending to rub the sore knee. He managed to make it into the restroom and took a seat in one of the stalls. Raising the leg of his dress pants, he pulled off his prosthesis and looked at the swelling knee. It appeared the skin had been pinched when the prosthesis was almost jarred loose.

Carefully, Jackie ran his fingers over the injury. The blood was blossoming just under the surface of the thin skin. He readjusted his stump sock and reattached his limb. Standing, he braced his hands on the wall as he worked through the pain.

Jackie took a deep breath and wiped the sweat from his brow as he checked himself in the mirror. He knew how upset his lover would be if he thought he'd hurt him. Trying to relieve a little of his tension, Jackie rocked his head from side to side, until he heard and felt a satisfying pop.

The door swung open and there stood a concerned Brier. "You okay?"

"Yeah. Just washing up." He turned and followed Brier from the room, biting the side of his cheek with each step.

Although he wanted nothing more than to get home and take off the prosthesis, Jackie reached for Brier's hand as they entered the parking lot. "You feel like running by a car lot or two on the way to the house?"

Brier's entire face seemed to light up at the words. "Really?"

Jackie used his key fob to unlock the doors as they neared. "Yep, really. As a matter of fact, why don't you drive us there?"

Getting behind the wheel, Brier held his hand out for the keys. After passing them over, Jackie pulled Brier's head in for a deep kiss. He knew if he tried to hold Brier back from becoming the man he wanted to be, his lover would bolt in a heartbeat. No, better to give Brier all the love he felt, and hope like hell he still needed him a month down the road.

* * * *

Brier couldn't get over the number of cars. "What does it mean, new and used?"

Instead of answering right away, Jackie opened the trunk and pulled out the crutches he hadn't used in a long time. "Jackie? Are you feeling okay?"

He'd noticed earlier that his boyfriend's face appeared paler than usual, but had quickly forgotten about it once Jackie said they were going car shopping.

"Yeah. I guess I'm a little tired. Thought I'd rely on these things while we shop around."

Brier watched Jackie struggle towards him. "Would you rather go home?"

Jackie stepped up to him and gave him a brief kiss. "Don't worry so much. I'm fine. Now. Let's find you a car."

"Okay," Brier agreed as they started down the first row. "So what's the difference between new and used?"

"Oh, about ten thousand dollars." Jackie chuckled. "Actually, a used car means that someone else has already owned it, driven it and most likely puked in it at one time or another."

Brier scrunched up his nose. "Did they clean it?"

Jackie laughed harder. "Yeah, truth is you won't see much difference between the new and used cars."

"Well, they're all really shiny."

Brier looked around the big parking lot. He saw a lot of cars that looked like the kind of four-door car Jackie drove. Maybe that's what he should go with? He walked towards a dark blue car. On the way, a bright shiny red Jeep caught his eye. Brier couldn't help but gaze at the sexy car.

"Sweet, isn't it?" A short guy with brown hair strode up and stuck out his hand. "The name's Jim Forkland."

"Nice to meet you, sir, I'm Brier, and this is my boyfriend Jackie."

He couldn't get over how friendly the man was, and they'd only just met. Brier glanced over his shoulder at Jackie as he shook Jim's hand. His eyes kept straying back to the tomato coloured four-wheel drive.

None of the men he knew drove cars that looked like the Jeep, they all had cars similar to Jackie's. Brier turned away from the temptation and pointed towards the sedan. "I think I should look closer at that one."

"Oh, well, okay. Hey, let me go ahead and get your name and phone number while we're looking."

"That won't be necessary unless we find something we really like," Jackie replied, before Brier could give Jim his information.

Brier stuck his hands in his pockets and walked around the dark blue car. He knew it was probably a really good car, because it had letters on the back with a fancy design, but it just didn't speak to him. Owning his own car had been a dream since he'd been out of the hospital. Once again, the red Jeep came to mind. That was the car he'd always wanted, but how did he tell Jackie?

"Hey, Jim," Jackie broke into Brier's thoughts as he called the salesman over. "Could we get the keys to that one over there? I think Brier needs to take it for a spin."

Brier turned to Jackie. "But it's not...like..."

"It's not like that boring sedan you're looking at. Who wants that? Go for the sexy one."

"But you have one with the four doors."

"Yeah, and it's boring as hell. That's a company car, Brier. If I had my pick, I'd go with the red."

Brier wanted to jump into Jackie's arms and kiss him right there in front of the salesman, only the crutches stopped him. Instead, he bounded over to gaze into his lover's eyes. "You sure?"

"Of course I'm sure. How're you supposed to know if this is the one for you if you don't test drive it?"

The salesman agreed and went to get the keys and something called a dealer plate. Brier didn't really know what that was, but he didn't care. He couldn't believe he was actually going to drive the shiny Jeep.

Jim came back and handed Brier a set of keys. "I'll have to ride along, of course, for insurance reasons."

"Okay." Brier would've agreed to almost anything at that point.

Brier helped Jackie stow his crutches in the car before they both climbed in. He buckled his seat belt and turned the key in the ignition. The sound the Jeep made as it came to life thrilled him. He grinned over at Jackie. "I think I'm in love."

Jackie smiled back and placed a hand on Brier's thigh. Brier pulled out of the parking lot and turned right. At the first stop light, he glanced down and was surprised to see he was hard. A quick check of the rear view mirror told him the salesman had no idea how much Brier was aroused by the Jeep.

"So what do you think?" Jim asked from the backseat.

"Yes, Brier, what do you think?" Jackie asked, squeezing Brier's thigh.

"I love it. I want it." He winked at Jackie.

"Good. Let's get back to the dealership so I can check under the hood for a few minutes before we discuss price." Jackie gave Brier knowing look. "The faster we can take care of this, the better."

"I agree," Brier chuckled.

* * * *

By the time Brier walked into the house, Jackie was already naked and in bed. "What took you so long?"

Brier grinned and started undressing. "Bram insisted he take the Jeep for a test drive to make sure it was safe."

Brier pushed his pants down and stepped out of them. Jackie's mouth began to water at the hardness bobbing between his lover's legs. "I think he just wanted to drive it though. Declan said Bram'll be buying one next."

"Turn off the light, babe," Jackie instructed. Although they usually made love with the lights on, he didn't want Brier to see his bruised and swollen knee. He had things other than pity and first aid on his mind.

The room was suddenly dark, save for the streetlight shining through the bedroom curtains. Jackie felt the bed dip, and moved his sore knee as far away as he could.

Brier started to chuckle when he felt how far apart Jackie's legs were spread. "Does this mean you want me to fuck you?"

"I figured it was your turn. You've opened yourself to my cock every night for the past week."

He pulled Brier into a kiss, thrusting his tongue inside the warmth of the man he loved. The Jeep had been an unexpected surprise, but it sure seemed to make Brier happy, and that was Jackie's goal in life. Hopefully, as long as he kept Brier happy, his lover would have no reason to stray.

Brier's hands began exploring Jackie's body, those beautiful long fingers tracing each ridge and dip. Jackie moaned as Brier's hand wrapped around his cock. He put his hands on Brier's shoulders and gave him a nudge. "Need to feel your mouth on me."

With a moan of agreement, Brier's mouth began working its way down Jackie's body. Closing his eyes, Jackie gave himself over to his lover's teeth and tongue. He loved the way Brier nipped gently at his skin before laving it.

Reaching over to the bedside table, Jackie's hand closed around the ever-present bottle of lube. Brier settled between Jackie's spread thighs and began running his tongue up the length of Jackie's cock. "Oh, yeah."

Brier groaned and swallowed Jackie's length. With the lube in one hand, Jackie used his other to bury his fingers in Brier's silky black hair as he began thrusting in and out of his lover's mouth. He was sorry the lights were out. Nothing in the world was sexier than watching himself fuck Brier's mouth.

Jackie was so turned on he forgot about his knee and tried to use both legs to thrust deeper. As soon as he put his weight on his stump, the pain seared through his entire leg and into his hip.

"Fuck," he yelled out in pain.

Brier's mouth popped off Jackie's cock. "I'm sorry. Did I hurt you?"

Jackie swallowed around the bile rising in his throat. He couldn't catch his breath as his knee continued to throb. "Turn on the light, babe."

Brier crawled up to the head of the bed and switched on the lamp. Sitting back on his haunches, he stared down at Jackie. "What's wrong?"

"My knee," Jackie panted through the pain.

Swinging back the sheet that covered Jackie's knee, Brier gasped. "Oh my God, what did you do?"

When Jackie didn't answer right away, Brier jumped out of bed and left the bedroom. Jackie heard the water running in the bathroom and the medicine cabinet open and close. He felt a sudden moment of pride that even without being told, Brier knew exactly what he needed.

Within seconds Brier was back. He had a glass of water, medicine bottle and cold washcloth in his hands. Shaking out two pills, Brier helped Jackie sit up enough to take them and swallow half the water in the glass. Next the cool rag was placed on Jackie's forehead.

"Hold on and I'll get that bag of peas from the freezer."

Brier once again raced out of the room. Lying there, Jackie couldn't help but wonder if the injury would set his therapy back. He was finally starting to get around pain-free again.

A naked Brier came back into the room and gently laid the ad-hoc ice pack on his knee.

"You should've told me," Brier pouted.

"I didn't want to upset you. Some things are better dealt with alone," Jackie tried to explain.

Brier curled up against him. "It's hard being a man sometimes, isn't it?"

"Yeah. We're supposed to be so strong and do things for ourselves, but it's not always easy."

"No, it's not," Brier mumbled, pushing his face against Jackie's neck.

Jackie wrapped both arms around his partner and kissed the top of his head. He could feel the pain medication taking effect and yawned. "I think I'm going to call in sick in the morning. Maybe a day off my feet will be enough to get me back on track."

Brier nodded. "No matter what, you know I love you, right?"

"Sure, babe." Jackie wondered where that had come from. "Something wrong?"

Brier shook his head. "I just want you to be proud of me, that's all."

"I'm proud of you every day." Jackie drifted off to sleep still puzzling Brier's mood.

Chapter Eight

The ringing phone woke Jackie from his mid-morning nap. He reached over and clumsily picked up the receiver. "Hello."

"How's the knee?" Mac asked.

"Not too bad as long as I don't walk on it, look at it or breathe on it," Jackie answered.

"Damn, you must've done a number on it."

"Yeah, something like that."

"You need me to find someone to take over your classes again tomorrow?" Mac asked.

"Yeah, as much as I hate it, I should probably stay in bed another day."

"What about Brier?"

"What about him?" Jackie rubbed his eyes as he started to drift back to sleep.

"Will he be gone again tomorrow?"

"Huh? What do you mean gone again? Isn't he there?" Jackie had a sinking feeling. It wasn't like Brier to miss a day of work, especially because Jackie had kissed him this morning before sending his lover out the door.

"No. He called in this morning and told me about your knee. Said he needed to take the day off. I just assumed he was taking care of you."

Flashes of Brier's strange mood the previous day came back to him. "Can you patch me through to Bram?"

"Sure, is there something wrong?" Mac asked.

"I sure as hell hope not."

"Hang on, I'll get Bram for you."

Jackie was put on hold. A thought struck him. Maybe Brier was just downstairs making him soup or something. He lifted himself enough to look out the window beside his bed. *Shit.* His sedan was the only vehicle in the driveway. His mind was whirling through possible scenarios until Bram came on the line.

"Hey, what's up?"

"Have you heard from Brier?"

"No. Why?"

Jackie sat up. He knew if Bram hadn't heard from his twin, it couldn't be good. "Brier left this morning. I thought he was going to work, but Mac just told me he called in."

"What? Where the hell's he at then?"

"Good question." Jackie fought back and forth with himself for several seconds before proceeding. "He was acting strange yesterday. I thought it was the car thing, but then when we got back to the house his mood seemed to continue."

"What kind of mood. Like a going-off-the-deep-end kind of mood?"

"No, I don't think so." He thought about Brier's bristly attitude in the accounting office. "Hell, I don't know. He seemed edgy and then last night he was talking about how hard it was to be a man..."

Jackie swallowed around the lump in his throat. "Fuck! How could I have misread him? Brier said he wanted me to remember that no matter what happened he loved me."

Images of Brier hurting himself came to mind. "You don't think he would do anything to himself..."

"Dammit! Don't fucking talk like that," Bram cursed, cutting him off.

Jackie hissed through his teeth as he swung his legs over the side of the bed. "Can you put me on hold and try and call his cell?"

"Hang on."

Hearing the familiar music of Brier's cell phone coming from the living room, Jackie groaned. The music eventually cut off and Bram came back on the line.

"No answer, but I left a message."

"He left his phone on the charger again," Jackie said, feeling totally defeated. "Maybe he's at the church? He told me yesterday he wanted to go by there, but then the whole car thing came up and I forgot."

"I'll go down the street and check."

"Okay. I'm gonna get dressed and head your way. Call me when you find something out."

"Will do," Bram answered before hanging up.

Jackie looked down at his swollen knee. He knew there was no way he'd be able to walk on it, so he didn't bother putting on his prosthesis. Standing, he balanced himself on one foot as he hopped over to the dresser.

With a pair of sweats and T-shirt in hand, Jackie used the furniture and walls to balance him as he made his way to the living room.

As he sat on the sofa to dress, he tried to remember where he'd left his crutches the night before. One of the first things he'd done when he came into the house was go to the kitchen for aspirin and a beer.

He slowly made his way to the kitchen. The white envelope with his name neatly printed on the front nearly stopped his heart. He collapsed in the kitchen chair and fingered the envelope resting neatly on the table. Was it a Dear John?

Before he could gather the nerve to open the envelope, the phone started to ring. Sliding his chair over enough to reach the phone on the wall, Jackie answered, already sure of what Bram had found.

"He's not there."

"Yeah, I didn't think so. There's a letter here on the kitchen table addressed to me," Jackie confided.

"What's it say?"

"I don't know. I haven't had the guts to read it yet."

"Well open it, man. I'm worried sick here."

Scooting himself back to the table, Jackie picked up the envelope and slid the single sheet of notebook paper out. He unfolded it. There were only five lines written on the page.

"Jackie," he began to read aloud.

"I hope you're not mad at me. I love you so much, but this is something I have to do. I made a bargain, and you and Bram always tell me a man is only as good as his word. If you don't want me anymore, turn off the porch-light, and I'll know I'm no longer welcome."

Jackie read the short note again. "What the fuck is that supposed to mean?"

Bram groaned. "He mentioned his bargain. The only one I know he's made is the one with God."

Jackie re-read the note with Brier's bargain in mind. "You don't think he went to talk to the prosecutor or one of the witnesses, do you?"

"That's exactly what I think," Bram answered.

"But he's never even driven out of the area. How's he supposed to drive all the way to Oklahoma by himself?"

"That's not the biggest question," Bram said.

"Yeah, and what's that?"

"How did he find out where to go in the first place?"

* * * *

Brier stopped at a gas station to pee and get something to eat. After taking care of business, he browsed the aisles for something that looked good. He'd already had three candy bars for breakfast, but he didn't know if he had enough cash on him to pay for the gas he'd need and a real lunch.

He spotted a sandwich wrapped in plastic in the refrigerated section and pulled the money out of his front jeans pocket. He still had a fifty and a twenty. He'd just filled his tank and knew that would cost him thirty-eight dollars, and the sandwich was three dollars. That would only leave him about twenty-nine dollars. What would he do if Jared refused to talk to him and he needed to drive all the way to Oklahoma? He'd definitely need more gas.

With a sigh, Brier bypassed the sandwich and grabbed a small bag of chips instead. At least he'd remembered to take a couple of bottles of water before leaving the house earlier. He may get hungry, but at least he should have enough for gas.

He paid for his stuff and got back into the Jeep. For some reason, he didn't like his new car nearly as much as he had the previous night. Even though he'd taken the soft-top off and had spent the day in the open air and sunshine, it almost felt suffocating. He wondered if it was because he felt so guilty about lying to Jackie.

He took out the map and studied it. He'd asked the man inside how much further to Lubbock and the man had said he was within twenty-three miles. His plan was to stop at another station once he got into Lubbock and ask someone how to get to Jared's address.

Pulling out of the station, Brier drove the remaining distance in a fog of mixed emotions. He thought about the letter he'd left for Jackie. Maybe he was doing this all wrong. What if God got mad at him for hurting Jackie?

By the time he pulled into the first gas station he saw, his cheeks were wet with tears. Address in hand, he got out of the Jeep and walked inside the small, dirty building. "Excuse me, sir, but could you tell me how to get to 1325 Oakmont?"

The nice man gave him directions, while Brier furiously scribbled them on his sheet of paper. "And could you tell me where the nearest church is that might be open?"

"Which denomination?"

"Huh?"

"Are you Catholic, Methodist, Baptist, what?"

Brier shrugged. "It doesn't really matter. I just want to talk to God. I don't think he cares which church I'm in."

The guy chuckled. "You're alright, man. Go down about a mile and take a left. There'll be one on your right hand side."

"Thanks."

Armed with directions to both the church and Jared's house, Brier decided to go to the church first. The big brick building was easy to find, and he pulled into the parking lot. Quietly opening the door, he stepped inside and made his way to one of the wooden benches towards the front.

Bowing his head, he spoke to God. "It's me, Brier. I'm in a different place than usual, but I figure you know that already. I had to come down here to talk to Jared. Remember I already told you about him. He was the guy that Rick hurt after he left the hospital I was in. By the sound of it, I was really lucky. Jackie told me Rick actually beat Jared up really bad when he threatened to tell on him. Rick never did that to me, but to be honest, God, I never thought of telling anyone until that day with Jackie."

Brier heard a noise behind him and glanced over his shoulder. A woman had come in and was watering the big plants in the back of the church. Turning back to the conversation at hand, Brier spoke even softer.

"I didn't forget about the deal I made with you when Jackie was sick. It's been a lot harder than I thought it'd be. As a matter of fact, that's kinda why I'm here. I'm really confused between doing what I think you want and doing what my heart wants. I don't know that I would be able to live without Jackie. He means everything to me, but so do you."

Brier sat with his head down for another thirty minutes. Drying his eyes, he decided he'd stop by Jared's house and try and talk to him. If Jared refused, he'd forget about convincing the others to go to court and drive back home to Jackie. What he realised while sitting there was that he had fulfilled his promise to God. He'd done everything in his power to see that Rick was in trouble for the things he'd done. Although his word alone hadn't been enough, it wasn't his fault. The really important thing was taking care of the love between him and Jackie. He knew God would see it the same way.

With a final nod to the altar, Brier went back out to his Jeep. He pulled out the piece of paper and followed the directions to an old, run-down white house. The scraggly brush in the front yard looked like it had never even been mowed or cut down.

Brier shook his head, suddenly feeling sorry for Jared. He'd been lucky. Having brothers like Bram and Thor had changed Brier's life dramatically. Brier didn't know if Jared had any family, but by the looks of the house he'd have to say either he didn't, or they didn't care about him.

Climbing out of the Jeep, Brier walked up the crumbling front walk to the small porch. He'd rehearsed what he wanted to say most of the five hour drive. Squaring his shoulders, Brier raised his fist and knocked on the door. The torn screen flapped with each tap of Brier's knuckles, reminding him once again of how little Jared seemed to have.

He could hear some shuffling around behind the screen door before a man finally appeared in front of him. Small in stature, with white blond hair, a pair of deep blue eyes stared out at Brier. "Can I help you?"

"Jared Grant?" Brier thought he detected bruising on the man's face earlier, but when the smaller man spoke, the split in his lip was quite clear.

"Are you okay?" Brier asked.

The man took a step back. "What do you want?"

"Are you Jared Grant?"

"Yes."

"I'm Brier Blackstone…"

Before he could go any further, Jared shook his head and tried to shut the door in his face. Knowing his chance to talk to the man was slipping away, Brier opened the screen door and blocked the door with his body. "Please. I just need to talk to you for a minute. I've come all the way from Albuquerque."

"I'm not supposed to talk to anyone." Jared's voice was so soft Brier could barely hear him.

With nothing between them, it was easier to see the bruises covering Jared's face, neck and arms. "Oh my God, who did that to you?"

The tip of Jared's tongue snaked out to touch against the fresh cut on his lip. "You have to leave. He'll be home any second," he spoke in a rushed fashion.

"Who?" Brier repeated.

Tears began to run down Jared's face. "He'll kill you if he finds you here."

"Who? Please, come with me. I can take you somewhere where you'll be safe from whoever's hurting you." He could see the desire to escape in Jared's eyes.

"I can't. I have a cat." Jared's eyes continued to search the street behind Brier. "You need to go now."

"I'm not leaving unless you come with me. We can take the cat if that's what you're worried about."

Jared shuffled from foot to foot. "I have a carrier."

Seeing the information as a good sign, Brier nodded. "Good, that's good. Go get it, grab your cat and let's go."

Jared's slim delicate finger lifted to run over his cut lip. "How can you promise he won't find me?"

"I work for a bodyguard agency. Their job is to protect people. We can help you."

Jared's blue eyes closed momentarily. When he opened them again, Brier saw a new resolve in the previously frightened man. "Okay. See if you can get Jelly Beans while I find her carrier."

Before he could say anything else, Jared turned and rushed through the house. Brier stepped further inside. He couldn't get over the interior of the place. Though everything appeared to be neat as a pin, Jared's poverty was evident everywhere he looked. No wonder the poor guy thought he had to put up with abuse.

He spotted a fluffy tail scurry behind a chair and knelt down on the threadbare carpeting. "Jelly Bean," he called.

"Come on girl," Brier coaxed. A cute little face with a pink nose peaked out.

"Hey, girl." Brier reached for the long-haired calico cat. With a loud meow, Jelly Bean snuggled against his chest.

"Found it," Jared proclaimed, running back into the room with a half-empty bag of cat food tucked under his arm and the carrier in his hands.

Brier took the carrier and managed to get Jelly Bean inside and headed for the door. "Okay, let's go."

"Hang on, I need to get something." Jared disappeared and Brier started to get nervous. "Come on, Jared!"

Out of breath, Jared came back into the room carrying a small box. "I'm ready."

They ran out of the house and towards the Jeep. Brier was buckling the carrier into the backseat when he heard screeching tires and a startled scream from Jared.

"He's back."

Brier clicked the seatbelt into its slot and stood. What he saw nearly dropped him to his knees. He looked from Jared to Rick. All the memories of abuse he suffered at the hands of the big orderly came rushing back.

Jared started to cry while trying to hide behind the Jeep.

"What the fuck is goin' on?" Rick bellowed, opening the door before he'd even put the old pickup into park.

"Oh no, oh no…" Jared continued to mutter in his crouched position.

"Get in the Jeep, Jared," Brier ordered, putting himself between the small battered man and his former abuser. Jared remained frozen until Jelly Bean meowed, trying to get out of her carrier.

The simple sound from his beloved cat seemed to help Jared make up his mind. Once he was in the passenger's seat, Brier tossed him the keys. "Lean over and start it up."

"Get outta that Jeep you perverted little fuck!" Rick screamed.

Brier noticed how Jared almost immediately started to follow Rick's orders, leaving no doubt of the control Rick had over him.

"Stay where you are, Jared. I'll take care of this."

Facing the demon, Brier squared his shoulders. "Don't you talk to him. I'm going to make sure you never hurt him again."

Rick started to cackle. "Really, fag? And how're you going to do that? You couldn't even protect that cherry ass of yours. How're you plannin' to protect a girlie man like ole Jared here?"

Brier heard the Jeep's engine come to life. Looking Rick in the eyes, Brier held his ground between the Jeep and Rick. "I'm not the same person I used to be."

"What, you mean you're not stupid anymore?" Rick laughed, stalking closer to Brier.

Brier could feel his fragile control begin to slip. Memories of his own mother calling him stupid came back to haunt him, as well as his hands wrapping around her neck until she took her last breath.

No. He told himself. *Think of Jackie. Think of all the real men you've come to know and love.* His breathing began to even out. He took several steps back towards the vehicle. He knew he didn't need to fight Rick to win this battle.

He spun quickly and jumped into the Jeep. Putting it into gear he stepped on the gas just as a meaty fist slammed into his jaw. Brier's head snapped to the side as he peeled away from the kerb.

Jared squeaked beside him. "Oh my God, are you okay?"

Brier rubbed his jaw as he watched Rick in the rear view mirror. Turning the corner, Brier headed out of town, but a quick glance in his mirror had him worried. "We can't make it like this," he yelled over the blowing wind. "Where's a police station?"

"No. We can't go to the police, he'll kill me."

Even though he knew Jackie would get mad at him, Brier took one hand off the wheel and reached for Jared's frail hand. "Listen to me. I promise you. Cross my heart. Nothing bad will happen to you."

Jared squeezed Brier's hand. "Turn right at the next light."

Chapter Nine

Mac had half the agency out looking for Brier, so the only thing for Jackie to do was sit home and worry. With his knee the way it was, actively searching for his lover wasn't an option. They had a team on the way to Tulsa, and one heading for Lubbock.

When his cell phone rang, Jackie prayed it was good news. He looked at the display on his phone and saw the Lubbock Police Department. *Shit.* "Hello?"

"Jackie?"

Jackie released the breath he wasn't even aware he'd been holding. Slumping back in the chair, he felt like crying. "Are you okay, babe?"

"Yeah. I'm so sorry I went behind your back," Brier apologised.

"You're safe aren't you?"

"For now, but I need you. I went to Jared's house, and he was bruised, and I could tell someone had been hitting him, and I told him he should leave with me, but he was really scared, and then there was Jelly Bean..."

"Brier, baby, take a deep breath and slow down. Who's Jelly Bean?"

"Jared's cat, but it's okay, because we managed to bring her with us when we got away from Rick."

Jackie's instincts kicked in and he bolted up from the chair, before collapsing to the floor. "Fuck!" he screamed as pain tore through his knee.

"Jackie," he heard Brier yell.

Putting the phone back to his ear, Jackie grunted. "I'm here, just hurt my knee again. Tell me what the hell Rick was doing there?"

"He'd been living with Jared, beating him up and...ya know, doin' stuff to him."

"Okay, so why are you calling from the police station?"

"Because Rick came when we were trying to leave and followed us. I didn't know what else to do, so I came here."

"You did the right thing, babe. Did the police go after Rick?"

"Yeah, they're looking for him now."

"Okay, sit tight. We've got a couple of guards headed that way anyway. I'll give them a call and send them your way."

"I can't leave my Jeep down here."

Jackie couldn't help but grin. Despite all the tension of the day and everything Brier had been through, his lover was still worried about his car.

"Have Merritt drive it back for you."

"And Jared and Jelly Bean?" Brier asked.

"They should be fine back in their house if they arrest Rick, right?"

Brier got very quiet on the other end of the phone. "Brier?"

"You didn't see how they lived, Jackie. Jared doesn't have anyone like I do to help look after him."

"So what're you asking?" Jackie loved the shit out of Brier, but he wasn't sure about taking on a houseguest with a cat.

"I don't know. I promised him I'd keep him safe." Brier seemed to cup his hand over the phone. "He's really scared. I think if we make him feel safe, I can get him to testify."

"Okay, he can stay with us for a few days until we can find him something," Jackie relented.

"Well I was thinking maybe he could stay in the dorm at the agency. I think he'd feel a lot safer there."

Even better. "I'll talk to Amir. He's in charge of the training facility."

Silence once again came from Brier's end. "Brier?"

"Yeah, I'm here. I just don't know what to say to you. I know what I did was wrong, but I'm glad I was able to help Jared."

"Me too, babe. Don't worry. I'm only a little mad at you. We'll work it out."

"I love you, Jackie."

"I love you too. I'll meet you guys at the training facility. It'll give me a chance to get a few things ready."

"Thanks."

Jackie could still hear the worry in his lover's voice. "Just get home so I can kiss that gorgeous face of yours."

Brier chuckled. "Not so gorgeous any more. Rick about broke my jaw when he punched me..."

Jackie's fist clenched tighter around the phone. The thought of Rick getting close enough to Brier to punch him didn't sit well at all. He'd promised Brier he'd never again be hurt by Rick.

Before he could reply to Brier's comment, his other line beeped. Pulling the phone away from his ear, he glanced at the display.

"Listen, babe, Bram's on the other line. I need to tell him you're safe. I'll meet you at the facility."

"Okay, bye, Jackie."

"Bye, babe."

Jackie ended the call and clicked over. "He's safe."

* * * *

"Another cup?" Seb asked.

Jackie drained the dregs of his coffee and handed his mug over. "Thanks."

Dammit. He couldn't sit there any longer. If it weren't for his knee, he would've headed towards Lubbock to pick up Brier himself. Other than getting things set up for Jared, he'd done nothing but worry.

He glanced over to where Bram and Declan were sitting. Bram had been on the phone with Thor non-stop since he'd heard the news. Jackie knew he'd be welcome to sit with them, but getting into any kind of argument with Bram wasn't worth it just then.

Seb took a seat next to him and handed over a fresh cup of coffee. "It's all my fault, ya know."

"What?"

Seb, who seemed as restless as Jackie, jumped up from his chair and started pacing the bottom-floor dorm lounge. "I'm the one who gave Brier Jared's address. He said they'd been friends in the hospital and he wanted to write to him."

Well, at least that answered one of the questions he was going to put to Brier. "Didn't you think it odd that he didn't ask me or Bram to get that information?"

"Yeah, and I asked him about that." Seb's black eyes shifted to the side. "He said the two of you didn't approve of his friendship with the guys from his past. I knew I was going behind your back giving it to him, but he's a hard guy to say no to."

"Tell me about it," Jackie mumbled.

He knew by the cat-like stance Seb was maintaining he was waiting for Jackie to let loose on him. "Relax. I'm not mad."

After a short nod, Seb continued pacing. Jackie was surprised the guy was so wound up. He knew Brier was friendly with the man, but he had no idea anyone could crack through Seb's shell to elicit such concern. He wondered how deep Seb's feelings for Brier ran.

"You got designs on my man?" he finally asked.

Seb stopped in his tracks and spun around. "What? No."

"Then why the over-the-top concern?" Jackie had dealt with a lot of men in this profession, and Seb was usually colder than any of them.

Seb shrugged and gazed out the window. "He reminds me of my own brother."

The statement further shocked Jackie. No one knew anything about Seb, other than he'd grown up in foster care. The fact that he'd let slip something about his personal life was definitely a first.

"How so?" Jackie prodded.

"Just does."

A car pulled up in front of the big window followed by Brier's Jeep. "That's them."

Jackie grabbed his crutches and got to his feet while Seb unlocked the security door. Jackie pulled out his phone and called Mac. "They're here."

"Okay, I'm trying to deal with a situation in Chicago right now, but I'll be over as soon as I can to check on them."

"Trouble in Chicago?"

"Yeah, and I think it's only the beginning. I've put the guys protecting Alec on alert as well. I think Lenny Constentine is flexing his muscles from jail."

"Shit. Okay, keep me posted." Although he wasn't involved in the Constentine mess any longer, both sets of agents protecting the members of the crime family were his friends.

Brier was the first one out of the car and through the door. Balancing his weight on his good leg, Jackie tossed down one of the crutches so he could wrap an arm around the man he loved.

The bruise on Brier's jaw started to raise his blood pressure until his man soothed him with a kiss. Damn, how he loved Brier's kisses. He swept the interior of Brier's mouth with his tongue wishing the two of them were already naked in their bed at home.

"Don't ever do that to me again," Jackie warned, breaking the kiss.

"Never," Brier agreed. Turning towards the door, he said, "Jared, come over here and meet my boyfriend."

Jackie focused on the small, battered man standing just inside the room. He appeared completely lost and bewildered as he clutched a cat carrier in his arms. Jackie couldn't believe this was the man he'd cussed so many times for being a coward. No wonder the man was too afraid to talk to the prosecutor.

Jared studied the room and the people in it, before walking towards them. Brier held out his hand, putting it on Jared's shoulder when he got close enough. "Jared, this is my boyfriend Jackie."

Jackie had to take his arm from around Brier to reach out to the man. "Nice to meet you."

Jared tried to balance the carrier under one arm, eliciting several meows from Jelly Bean, before finally setting it on the ground in front of his feet. "Nice to meet you, too. Brier's told me a lot about you."

Jackie zeroed in on the scars running up Jared's wrists. The prosecutor had never divulged why Jared had been in a mental hospital, but Jackie had a pretty good idea. He shook the man's hand gently and motioned for Seb.

"I'd like you to meet a friend of ours, Sebastian James."

"Call me Seb," Seb corrected, shaking Jared's hand.

Without letting go of Jared's hand, Seb leaned closer to the man and practically growled. "Who did that to you?"

Jared quickly pulled his hand away and took several steps back, fear in his eyes. Brier immediately went to Jared and stood in front of him, blocking Jackie's view of the frightened man. The two of them spoke quietly for several moments before Brier turned back to Seb.

"I'm going to help Jared and Jelly Bean get settled in their room. Can you tell me which one?"

Jackie glanced at Seb. The man's jaws were clenching, showing his apparent anger. He wondered if he should have Jared moved to another wing. Seb had offered to look after their new arrival, so Jared had been given the room next to his, but now Jackie was questioning that decision.

"Room 217," Jackie finally said when Seb remained silent.

Brier gave Jackie another kiss before picking up the cat carrier. "Where's your box of stuff?"

"Johnny carried it in," Jared informed Brier.

"Why don't you go get it from him, and I'll hold Jelly Bean."

Jackie noticed the way Jared took several steps backward before finally turning around. He'd known men like that, men who were leery of turning their backs to people. Jared's scars ran deeper than the ones on his skin.

Once Jared was far enough away, Brier addressed Seb. "Don't think he doesn't like you. He's afraid of almost everyone."

"Who did that to him?" Seb asked again.

"Rick Sutcliff. The same guy who hurt me. He must've followed Jared when he was released from the hospital." Brier shook his head. "I got away from Rick, but Jared wasn't strong enough."

Jackie noticed the way Seb's hands fisted at his sides. "Where's this Rick Sutcliff now?"

"The police caught him before he was able to get out of Lubbock."

"Lucky for him," Seb mumbled.

Jared appeared at Brier's side holding a small wooden box. "I need a bowl for Jelly Bean's water."

"Okay. All the rooms have a tiny kitchen in the corner, so there should be some bowls there," Brier assured Jared.

Jackie watched as Brier led Jared towards the elevator. "I'm not sure how he's going to do here. Maybe we should talk him into going back to the hospital for a while."

"He'll be fine. Now that I know some of what he's gone through, I'll be better able to handle the situation. I'll make sure he's okay," Seb replied, watching the two men step onto the elevator.

"Until you're called off on your next assignment. Do me a favour and don't get attached. I've seen what happens when you're forced to leave someone you care about."

"Don't worry. I don't attach myself anymore. That's why I'm in this business."

Jackie hid his grin by bending over to pick up his fallen crutch. By the ferocity in which Seb reacted to Jared's bruises, Jackie would guess the man was already more attached than he was aware.

* * * *

Watching Brier sleep, Jackie thanked God once again that he'd been returned safely. He had to admit, Brier had done a damn good job of handling the situation with Jared and Rick. He knew standing up to his abuser hadn't been easy, but from their talk the previous night, Brier was happy he'd done it.

Of course they still needed to convince Jared to testify, but with the frail, battered man now safe, Jackie had a feeling it would be much easier. The pictures Brier told him the police had taken of Jared would also go a long way in getting Rick locked up. If nothing else, the assault on Brier would get Rick some time in the pokey.

Jackie smiled thinking about Rick at the mercy of the guys in prison. It would serve the fucker right if they used Rick as their bitch. Turning the tables never sounded so satisfying.

Brier's eyelids fluttered several times before opening fully. "Morning."

Finally free to touch, Jackie ran his hand down Brier's side to smooth across his nude hip. "Morning, babe."

"What time is it?" Brier asked.

"Almost nine."

Brier's eyes popped open. "I need to get up. I'm late for work." Although he said it, Brier didn't move a muscle.

"I've already called in and told them you'll be late. Things are so crazy at the office they probably won't even miss you."

"Why, what's going on?"

"Someone broke into the Constentine mansion last night and nearly got to Addy. Mac's hot to say the least. I'd be surprised if the Black Dog Four unit gets out of this one with their asses intact."

Jackie's hand wandered to the morning erection poking him. "Mmm, something else's finally awake."

Brier grinned, ducking his head as Jackie started to stroke the cock in his hand. As the blood continued to fill the beautiful shaft, Jackie rubbed his fingers over the thick veins. If he didn't know better, he'd think Brier preferred getting a hand job more than an ass fucking.

Brier's moans filled the room as he began thrusting his hips in earnest. Jackie's own cock was leaking so much pre-cum it was pooling at the base of his shaft before running down his hip and onto the sheets below. "Need you."

Opening his eyes, Brier bit his lip. "I don't want to hurt your knee."

Jackie grinned. Leave it to his lover to be concerned about him even in the midst of passion. "I guess you'll have to give up your turn at my ass and ride me instead."

Brier practically jumped over Jackie to grab the lube on the nightstand. By his obvious enthusiasm, Jackie took it the arrangement was just fine with his lover. He knew Brier preferred to be on the receiving end of their lovemaking, which was just fine with Jackie most of the time.

While he was stretched out over him, Jackie didn't miss the opportunity to lick the head of Brier's cock. Damn, the man's pre-cum was sweet. Jackie suspected it was all the fruit his lover ate.

Brier braced his hands on the mattress and took several seconds to fuck Jackie's mouth before resuming his position beside him. After handing the bottle to Jackie, Brier got on all fours and turned around.

Jackie had to reach down and squeeze the base of his cock to stem off impending orgasm at the site of Brier's pretty hole. "Damn, babe, that looks good enough to eat."

With a wiggle of his ass, Brier scooted back enough for Jackie to reach him. "Breakfast is served."

Leaning up on his elbow, Jackie tasted the puckered skin before zeroing in with the tip of his tongue. He prodded the rosette for several seconds before Brier's body opened for him. Brier's entire body started to move as he fucked himself on Jackie's tongue.

Although his lover seemed to be enjoying himself, Jackie needed more, and his cock was in complete agreement. Balancing himself on one elbow, he managed to get the top off the lube. Holding the bottle above Brier's crack, Jackie let the slick fluid dribble down the channel towards its ultimate goal.

He quickly snapped the top back on and tossed the bottle back onto the bed. Using his thumb, Jackie began massaging Brier's hole. Moans of pleasure echoed through the bedroom as Jackie easily slipped two fingers inside Brier's ass. "You like this?"

"You know I do." Brier pulled away and turned to straddle Jackie's hips. "But I need more."

Reaching behind himself, Brier guided the crown of Jackie's cock to his hole. With a grunt and a sigh, his lover slowly impaled himself.

Jackie bit the inside of his cheek as Brier's body enveloped his shaft. He lifted his hands and pinched both dark brown discs on Brier's chest, pleased when the tiny nubs pebbled.

Catching Brier's gaze, Jackie smiled, seeing the love in the other man's eyes. He wanted to see that look for the rest of his life. Even if Bram continued to question his staying power, Jackie knew the truth. It had nothing to do with how smart Brier was or wasn't, and everything to do with the man's capacity to love and be loved.

SEB'S
SURRENDER

Dedication

Thanks, Theresa A., for all you do for me. I wouldn't be half as organised or productive without you.

Chapter One

Jared Grant pulled his thin jacket tighter around him and walked into the cold, blowing wind of a cloud-covered Albuquerque evening. He was so intent on getting to work on time, he didn't notice the car that pulled up beside him until a horn honked.

Jared jumped and spun around, ready to run. The driver of the shiny black El Camino SS rolled down his window.

"What're you doing out here?" Sebastian James asked.

Jared took a tentative step towards the car, truck, whatever it was. "Going to work."

Seb sighed and put the car in park. "Get in."

Jared opened the door and a blast of heat warmed him within seconds. He buckled his seatbelt and waited for Seb to pull away from the kerb. "It's just up here another six blocks."

"Yeah, I know where it is. Mind telling me what the hell you're doing walking to work in this weather?"

Confused by the man's anger, Jared inched closer to the passenger door. "Um...going to work?"

"Are you asking me?"

"Huh?" Seb confused Jared more than anyone he'd ever been around.

"You do that a lot, you know."

"Do what?"

"Make statements into questions. It's the lilt up on the end of your sentences, like you're not sure if you're going to work or not."

"Oh. Yes, I'm going to work."

Seb shook his head and pulled back into traffic. "So why are you walking instead of catching a ride?"

"Brier went home sick."

"So why not ask someone else?"

Jared tried to concentrate on the questions, but he kept getting distracted by Sebastian's dangerous-looking beauty. "I don't know anyone else well enough to bother."

With a disgusted sigh, Seb reached into the pocket of his black leather jacket and handed Jared a business card. "Call me when you need a ride. If I'm not on a job, I'll take ya."

Jared read the black and red printed business card. It listed Sebastian James as a security specialist and gave his phone number. "What's a security specialist do?"

"Whatever needs doing. Mostly I assess situations and make recommendations on the level of security a specific job requires."

Sebastian pulled into the small gas station parking lot. Jared opened the door, glancing back at the handsome man. "Thanks for the ride."

Seb reached out and grabbed Jared's arm. Out of reflex, Jared tried to jerk his arm back and lowered his head. Sebastian released his grip with a growl of what sounded like irritation. "How late're you working?"

"I don't get off until two."

"In the morning?"

Jared nodded his head. He knew his job sucked, but beggars couldn't be choosers. "It's the only shift they had available."

Seb rubbed his hands over his face. Jared could tell he irritated the man, but he wasn't the one who'd asked for a ride. "Call me, and I'll pick you up. You've got no business being on the streets that late."

Jared walked home from work every night at that time. He wondered why he was suddenly being told he had no business doing it. As grouchy as Seb acted, Jared doubted the man would appreciate a wakeup call at two. Instead of arguing, he stuffed the card into his jacket pocket and got out of the car. "Thanks again for the ride."

He walked into the store and acknowledged the older woman behind the counter. Mrs. Bell seemed nice enough, but she was the nosey type and Jared preferred to keep the skeletons in his closet safely locked away.

Jared stowed his jacket under the counter and watched out the window as Seb pulled out of the parking lot. Why had he waited so long? Jared shook his head. In the three weeks since he'd come to Albuquerque with Brier, Sebastian seemed to run hot and cold where he was concerned.

Seb was the one who'd insisted Jared file assault and rape charges against Rick Sutcliff, but since then, it seemed like Seb could barely stand to be around him. Jared couldn't help but to think Seb was disgusted by him now that he knew everything Rick had done to him.

Even thinking of Rick had Jared's stomach clenching into knots. It had been bad enough that Rick terrorized and raped him, Brier and Peter while in the hospital, but then Rick had showed up on his doorstep in Lubbock demanding to be let in.

Jared had been so afraid of the man, he'd done as he was told. From that day until Brier came knocking on his door, Rick had made his life a living hell. It was the lowest point of his twenty-five years, which was saying a lot.

He glanced down at the long straight scars running up both wrists. Even the events that had pushed him into trying to end his life hadn't been nearly as hard as the punishment Rick doled out on a daily basis.

"I'm off," Mrs. Bell called, grabbing her purse from the locked cabinet under the counter.

"Have a good evening."

Officially on the job, Jared took out his hideous smock and put it on. Some nights were harder than others, but Fridays and Saturdays sucked. He knew he shouldn't complain, even to himself. Getting the clerk job in the first place hadn't been easy.

Without a high school diploma or a work history, Jared knew the owner was taking a real chance hiring him. Jared had promised the kind man to be the best employee in the store, and he tried on a daily basis to keep his word. The drunks who stumbled in near midnight always put him on edge, but he often bluffed his way through it.

It didn't matter what he had to endure. For the first time in his life he was making his own money. He was finally free of his abusive parents, the hospital where they'd kept him for so long, and the man who'd almost succeeded in completely erasing what little humanity Jared had left.

He smiled as a customer stepped up to the counter. He may be wearing an ugly smock and doing a job he hated, but at least he was safe to live his life on his own terms. Could his life possibly get any better than that?

* * * *

Seb watched to make sure Jared got inside the store safely before pulling out of the lot. He still couldn't believe the man would walk over two and a half miles in the cold with a jacket at least two sizes too small.

He reached in his pocket and retrieved his phone.

"Hello?"

"Hey, Jackie, is Brier there?"

"He's sleeping. Why, what do you need?"

"I need to know why the hell no one's bothered to get Jared a decent coat. I just found him walking to work with that pitiful excuse for a jacket he has."

"Walking? Shit. I didn't even think about him going to work when I took Brier home early."

"Yeah. That's something else I'm not real happy about."

"Hey, man, Brier's my priority, not Jared. He's a nice kid, but there are times I have my hands full with my own business."

Seb pulled into his parking spot and turned off the engine. He knew Jackie was right. Although Brier had helped Jared get away from Rick, neither of them had taken Jared to raise. "Sorry. I guess seeing him walking beside the road like that just got to me."

"By the way, Brier offered to buy Jared some clothes, but he flatly refused. You know Brier, he didn't want to hurt Jared's feelings by pointing out the fact his wardrobe was lacking."

Seb had noticed Jared seemed to wear the same holey jeans and T-shirt almost every day, but he figured it was more a want than a need. "Maybe I'll run by the thrift store and pick him up a few things."

"I'm sure Brier would appreciate it. Not so sure about Jared though."

"Leave that to me. It's the reason I'm not buying him new clothes." After saying his goodbye, Seb started the El Camino and headed towards the thrift store on the other side of town.

He knew what it was to be too proud to ask for what was needed. Maybe he could get Jared to understand what had taken him years to figure out. There was nothing wrong with asking for help from your friends.

Where the hell had that come from? He barely knew Jared. He certainly wouldn't call the younger man a friend. Seb knew in any other circumstance, he probably would have already had the cute little blond in his bed, but Jared definitely wasn't someone to mess with. The blue eyed beauty made Seb feel too many things to allow him to get that close.

* * * *

Seb was in a dead sleep when his alarm clock woke him. He reached over and automatically smacked the snooze button, affording himself another ten minutes. He picked up his dream almost immediately and groaned as the rose coloured lips sucked his balls before moving up to engulf his cock.

"Do it, baby," he groaned, grinding his cock against the mattress.

His dream lover somehow managed to swallow Seb's cock to the root, which he knew from past lovers was no easy feat.

"That's it. Take it all." Seb wound his fingers around the near-white strands of hair as his lover continued to bob up and down on his length.

He felt the signs of his imminent release when the alarm clock once again disrupted his sleep. Slapping once again at the snooze button, it finally registered why he'd set the alarm in the first place. "Shit."

He sat up and rubbed the sleep from his eyes. It wasn't until he reached for his jeans he remembered the blond-haired head bobbing up and down on his cock. "Ahh, fuck."

Having dreams about Jared definitely wasn't allowed. It would be hard enough chauffeuring the guy around without dipping his finger in the honey pot. Dreams? Not going to help his control one bit.

Still half asleep, Seb pulled on his boots and shrugged into his jacket. He grabbed his keys off the small kitchen counter on the way out the door. Stepping outside into the cold air, he shivered and quickly got into his car. He wished he had the luxury of letting the car warm up, but he was late as it was.

Seb pulled out of the parking lot and headed towards town. A glance at the clock on the cassette player told him it was already twenty after two. "Shit."

He stomped on the accelerator, and almost immediately saw the flashing red and blue lights of a city police vehicle riding his ass. With a groan, Seb pulled over to the side of the road and turned off the engine. He reached into his back pocket and came up empty. *I'll be a sonofa...*

A tap sounded on the glass and Seb rolled down his window. "Evening."

"License and registration, please."

Seb reached over to the glove box, extracted his registration papers and handed them to the policeman. "Sorry officer, I seemed to have left my wallet at home. I was just going..."

"Is this the correct name?" the officer asked, gesturing to the papers.

"Yes. I work at Three Partners Protection."

"Just a minute." The officer walked back to his car.

Seb just knew the asshole was going to give him a ticket. Movement in front of him caught his eye. Jared walked to the driver's side window.

"Trouble?" he asked.

"Forgot my wallet. I'll probably get a ticket."

Jared looked at the police car and smiled. "No you won't."

Seb watched in his rear view mirror as Jared approached the police car. He couldn't hear what was being said, but both men ended up laughing. The officer got out of the car and approached Seb's window as Jared climbed into the passenger seat.

The cop handed Seb's registration over. "Watch your speed and grab your wallet next time."

After the officer walked back to his car and pulled back onto the road, Seb looked at Jared. "What the hell did you say to him?"

"That you were my friend who insisted I was too frail to walk the two and a half miles back to the dorm."

"And that worked?"

Jared grinned. "I know him. I give him free coffee and donuts when he comes into the store."

Seb couldn't get over the difference in Jared's face when he smiled. Already gorgeous, the younger man practically radiated angelic light with a flash of those shining white teeth and big blue eyes.

Jared yawned as Seb pulled away from the kerb. "Thanks for picking me up."

"You didn't call," Seb grumbled.

Jared yawned again. "I'm used to walking home, and I didn't want to wake you up."

Seb's hands gripped the steering wheel even tighter. The thought of Jared walking alone, down the country road towards the training facility dorms, bothered him. The convenience store was at the edge of town, but once you reached the limits, the sidewalks disappeared. The thought of some drunk ploughing Jared down on his way home from a bar, sickened him.

"It's getting cold."

"Yeah," Jared agreed. "When I think of New Mexico, for some reason cold doesn't come to mind."

"It gets this cold in Lubbock."

"You're right, but Texas doesn't have Mexico in its name."

Seb chuckled. He parked the El Camino SS in its usual spot and got out. Jared joined him in front of the door, and Seb tapped his security code into the pad. He heard the locks disengage and held the door open for Jared.

"I did a bit of shopping at the thrift store in town. I needed some more long-sleeve T-shirts. Anyway, I picked up a few things for you while I was there." Seb waited for the protest he knew was coming.

"I can't take them. I don't get paid for another week."

The elevator doors opened and Seb stepped in behind Jared. He knew he couldn't make a big deal out of the clothes. If Jared thought Seb was trying to give him a hand out, it would never work. After pushing the button for their floor, he shrugged. "Whatever. You might want to look at them though. They had a good sale going on for some reason. I got a pretty big bag of stuff for twenty-seven bucks. I don't mind waiting for the money until you get paid."

Jared didn't say anything as they got off the elevator and walked towards their assigned studio apartments. At his door, Jared dug his key out of his pocket. "I don't know. I still haven't been able to find out how much this room's gonna cost me, and I already owe Brier and Jackie for the groceries they've brought over."

As soon as Jared opened the door, Jelly Bean, his long-haired calico came out to rub against his legs. Seb reached down and gave the little lady a scratch behind the ears. "Let me run over and get the bag. You can try stuff on, see what you think."

Before Jared could protest, Seb had his key in the lock and opened his door. He grabbed the two plastic sacks just inside and followed Jared into his small apartment. Unlike Seb's studio, Jared's was devoid of any personal touches. The plain brown sofa and chair that came with the room depressed him.

Seb handed over the bags. "One has some jeans and shirts, the other a coat," he said in a casual tone.

Jared looked at the closed bags for several moments before pulling the bright red down-filled coat out. His eyes lit up, and Seb knew he'd chosen wisely.

"By the way, I'm sure the partners won't charge you much for rent. Mine's built into my salary. This entire floor's employee housing. When you have a job like mine, you're usually not in one place long enough to justify the cost of a real house or apartment."

Jared looked confused. "What do you mean a real apartment? This is nicer than anything I've ever lived in."

Seb knew from Brier what the living conditions for Jared had been in Lubbock. He swallowed around the foot lodged in his mouth. "Anyway, what I was trying to say is that these rooms aren't meant for students, so Mac, Amir and Nicco aren't losing any money by letting you stay in one."

Jared's gaze was still on the coat he held in his hands. The expression on the smaller man's face bothered Seb more than he cared to admit. "Well, uh, I'll get out of here and let you get some sleep. The receipt's in the bag, and I got them to throw in some wire hangers in case you want to keep them. Like I said, pay me when you can, I won't strong arm you if you have to wait until the end of the month."

Seb turned to leave.

"Thanks. You know, for the ride and the clothes."

Seb could tell by the soft tone of Jared's voice the gestures meant more to him than what they actually were. "You're welcome."

He got out of the apartment before he said something he'd regret. He'd given the guy a ride and a bag of used clothes, yet Jared spoke as if Seb had handed him the keys to a brand new car.

As he let himself in to his own studio apartment, he looked around at the top of the line furnishings he'd brought in to replace the generic shit that came with the place. His transformation into the man who had a couple of grand to drop on a couch had been so slow he hadn't noticed how much he'd really changed.

There was a time when an actual mattress to sleep on would have seemed like a dream. Seb pulled off his jacket and tossed it across the back of the expensive black leather sofa. There were times he wanted to remember every moment of the hell he'd endured as a child. The memories of scrounging the neighbourhood garbage cans for food for him and his brother, Alexander, helped him appreciate what he had. The images of a sick and mentally handicapped Alexander being driven away by a social worker, helped strengthen the walls he'd erected.

Being around Jared made him both want to remember and try to forget. Although Jared's situation was still largely unknown to Seb, he knew what it felt like to have someone offer kindness without expecting something in return.

The first time Seb had experienced it was in the Army. His commanding officer was a genuine, grade A asshole. One Thanksgiving, the hard-nosed man had invited Seb to join him and his family for a day of eating and football. It was the first normal Thanksgiving Seb had ever experienced and he'd sat all day with the family expecting them to ask his help putting a new roof on the house, or something similar. In his world, nothing was free. Nothing was given without expecting payment in one form or another.

Seb thought about the upcoming Thanksgiving holiday. He wondered if Jared would be spending it with Brier and Jackie? Amir, Nicco and Mac had already invited Seb along with several other bodyguards to their place. Maybe he should ask Mac if he could bring Jared along.

Jared spending the holiday alone wasn't an option. One way or another, Seb would make sure Jared wasn't stuck in his room, eating a turkey pot pie with only Jelly Bean for company.

* * * *

After he'd tried on the clothes, Jared sat at the small table and added the twenty-seven dollars to his IOU column. He knew he'd be lucky to make two hundred dollars on payday and he already owed Brier ninety-two dollars for groceries for the previous three weeks.

He needed to talk to Mac, Amir or Nicco about his rent. Despite what Seb said, he wouldn't stay without paying something. From the look of his budget though, he doubted he'd be able to give the partners more than three fifty and that was if he was lucky to maintain at least forty hours a week at work.

Jared's gaze once again wandered to the stack of clothes. Had he ever had so many? He knew he should probably take some of them back, but... His eyes landed on the red coat. Jared couldn't keep the smile off his face. How long had it been since he'd actually had a winter coat and a red one was icing on the cake.

Maybe he could pay Seb half when he got paid and the other half out of his next cheque? He stood and walked over to the clothes. Even he knew they should be washed before he wore them. Without the money for the laundry room downstairs, he'd need to do them all by hand.

With a shrug, Jared picked up the stack of six shirts and carried them into the bathroom along with the small bottle of detergent Brier had brought him. If he hung the shirts near the heating vents he might get lucky by having something new to put on the next day.

The thought made him smile. He couldn't believe how rich he'd become since Brier had knocked on his door.

Chapter Two

"Wake up."

Seb jerked and straightened in his chair to the sight of a grinning Mac. "Sorry."

Mac sat on the corner of Seb's desk and crossed his arms over his chest. "What's up with you lately? I've noticed you haven't been your normal cheerful self."

Seb snorted. He'd never been cheerful in his life. "I've been picking Jared up from work. Guess the change to my sleep pattern has me more out of sorts than usual."

"Doesn't he work the night shift?"

"Evenings. He gets off at two in the fucking morning." Seb scratched at his beard. He hadn't had the energy for a couple of days to trim his beard or shave his cheeks and neck.

"And you've been staying up every night to get him?"

Seb shook his head. "I've been trying to catch a few hours of sleep before and after I get him."

Mac stood. "Let me talk to Nicco and Amir. I'm sure there's a better solution."

"Thanks. I've been meaning to ask if I can invite him to Thanksgiving. I talked to Brier and he, Jackie, Bram and Declan are headed to Oklahoma to be with Thor's family."

"Sure, bring him along." Mac headed towards the door.

"By the way, has Jared asked you about paying rent?"

"He's asked. I keep dodging the question."

"He won't give up. It's important to him, and it's good for his self-esteem."

Mac stood in the doorway leading to the hall. "So tell me what I should tell him?"

"The best way would be to actually sit down and figure out how much it's costing Three Partners to house a person. Tell him you don't intend to make a profit, but give him a figure he can trust as the truth."

Mac nodded. "I'll see what I can come up with."

Seb stretched as Mac disappeared. It took him a moment to figure out what he'd been doing when he'd fallen asleep. Remembering, he picked up the phone.

"Archer."

"Hey, it's Seb. Where're you at?"

"Phoenix. Soaking up the sunshine. Why?"

"Slap on your earmuffs and get to Albuquerque. I might have a job for you."

"I just got off a job," Archer growled.

"Hey, if you don't want to live like a rock star for the next few months it's no skin off my nose."

"Babysitting? You know I hate those gigs. Besides, the holidays are coming up."

"It's for Keifer Zane." Seb sat back and waited. Keifer was one of the hottest rock stars out there. He'd also recently come out of the closet.

Archer whistled. "Damn. Is he getting backlash?"

"He's getting too much attention from both sides of the fence. There are some who want him dead and others who want him wed, to them, if you get my drift."

Seb knew Archer may very well blow up over what he had in mind, but it was the only way in Seb's opinion. "Just get here. We can discuss the details then."

Archer was still grumbling when he hung up. Seb sat back in his chair and grinned. Archer was more than a fantastic bodyguard, he also happened to be the only guy in Three Partners' employ who could pass as a rock star himself.

The leanly muscled, six-foot man was specifically trained in close quarters security. Archer was the kind of guy you wanted to have your back. With his blond, spikey hair and the light brown soul patch under his lip, Archer didn't look like the typical bodyguard.

Seb thought Archer would be the perfect choice to fool the media and fans into thinking he was simply Keifer's new boyfriend. It was Keifer's feeling that it was someone within his entourage that had outed him to the media for a chunk of money.

Once Archer accepted the job, he'd be seen on Keifer's arm at every available opportunity. The hope was that Archer would not only be able to root out the

Judas, but keep Keifer safe from the new onslaught of interested men.

Seb set the file aside and went to the next. He tried to concentrate on the papers in front of him, but soon his eyes began to close. God, he hoped Mac came up with a safe solution for Jared because his job was really starting to suffer.

* * * *

Jared was sprawled on the couch watching television when there was a knock at his door. He jumped up, secretly happy to have a visitor. Opening the door, he stared at the man standing in the hall. He'd met George a few times, but didn't really know him.

"Hi."

George smiled and bent down to pet a curious Jelly Bean. "I noticed this stuff had been in your mailbox the last couple of days, so I thought I'd bring them."

"I have a mailbox?"

George chuckled. "Sure. It's to the right of the entrance. Your room key opens it."

"So how did you open it?"

George's grey eyebrows bounced up and down. He handed the small stack of envelopes to Jared. "Because I'm the one who sorts the mail."

"Thanks." Jared picked up Jelly Bean, cradling the sweet cat in his arms.

George gave Jared a teasing salute and turned to walk back down the hall. "I put your name on your box, by the way."

"Thanks again." Jared shut the door and looked at the mail. He still couldn't believe he had letters. Who the heck did he know who'd even write one, and how did they find out where he...

Jared dropped the letters. As they fluttered to the floor, he caught sight of his name and the address of the dormitory. The handwriting was all too familiar. A knock on the door made him jump.

"Jared?" Seb called through the door.

Jared quickly kicked the offensive mail under the couch. After several calming breaths, he picked up the ever-curious Jelly Bean and opened the door. "Hi."

Seb's head tilted to the side. "You okay?" he asked as he reached out to scratch the cat behind her ears.

"Yeah." He took a step back in case Seb wanted to come in. While he waited for Seb to tell him what he wanted, Jared's gaze went back to the couch, hoping none of the envelopes were in view.

Seb's eyes followed Jared's, narrowing, as if he knew Jared was up to something. "I came by to invite you to Thanksgiving at Mac's tomorrow. A bunch of us have been invited."

"Me? Really?" Jared didn't want to admit he'd never understood the appeal of the holiday. Growing up, Thanksgiving had been yet another excuse for his parents to get drunk and mean.

"Yes. You. Mac said dinner will be served around two, but he invited us over early to watch the football game." Although Seb was speaking, he continued to study the small apartment with his eyes.

"I have to work my regular shift tomorrow."

"You're working Thanksgiving?"

"Sure. I'm the low man on the totem pole. But don't worry. I won't pull you away from your party to take me." For some reason the holiday seemed like a big deal to Seb. Jared wouldn't do anything to ruin it for him. Seb had been more than nice to him, even if the man did get grumpy on occasion.

"I'll pick you up at eleven. You should have more than enough time to enjoy dinner before *I* take you to work."

Jared bit his bottom lip. "Will there be drinking there?"

"You mean booze? Probably. Why?"

Once again, Seb gave Jared that narrow-eyed stare like he was trying to see into his soul. Jared knew he needed to do some thinking about the situation. His bruises had finally faded. He actually liked not being ashamed of the way he looked when he ventured out in public. "Can I let you know?"

Seb rested his hand on the wall beside Jared and leaned towards him. "What aren't you telling me?"

With the handsome man so close, Jared became flustered. Did Seb suspect he'd received mail? Or was his uneasiness about the holiday showing through? Maybe he could pick up an extra shift at the gas station?

When Seb leaned in further, Jared pressed against the wall. "N...nothing. I just want to check on my hours before I commit to anything."

With a grunt that told Jared the bigger man didn't believe him, Seb straightened. "I'll pick you up later for work."

Jared nodded.

With one last glance around the apartment, Seb turned and walked out. Jared shut the door and let out the breath he'd been holding. He noticed the half-hard cock pressing against the fly of his jeans. What the heck was up with that?

* * * *

Seb parked in front of Jackie's house and got out. When he'd finished with Jared, he knew he needed some answers. A quick call to Brier, and he was informed they were getting ready to leave for Oklahoma. Seb had asked if they could wait long enough for him to stop by for a few minutes and here he was.

As he walked towards the front door, Seb's mind was whirling. How was he supposed to watch over Jared when he knew so little about him?

The front door opened before he could even knock.

"Hi," Brier greeted, giving Seb a hug.

Seb didn't accept that sort of thing from most people, but Brier reminded him so much of Alexander, he couldn't push him away. "Sorry to hold you up, but I need to talk to you about Jared."

Brier led Seb into the living room. "Is there something wrong with him?"

Seb sat in one of the chairs and shrugged his shoulders. "I don't know. There's something going on with him, but I can't put my finger on it. I thought it might help if I knew a little more about him."

"Like what?" Brier asked, smiling when Jackie came into the room and sat beside him.

"I think I know as much as I need to about his life with Rick, but what about before then?"

Brier's brows knitted together. "You mean the hospital?"

Seb shook his head. "Before that. Do you know anything about his life growing up?"

Brier looked at Jackie. The two men seemed to have a silent discussion with their eyes before Jackie finally nodded. Brier turned back to address Seb. "He tried to kill himself."

"Yeah. I saw the scars. I assumed that's what put him into the hospital where Rick and the others began abusing him."

Brier began rubbing at the side of his head. It was something Seb noticed Brier did a lot when he was anxious about something.

"I don't know much. But he's mentioned a few things."

"Like?"

"When I told him the story of what happened to me to make me stupid…"

"Hey," Jackie cut in. "We don't use that word."

Brier smiled and kissed his partner. "I'm sorry."

Seb had heard the story of how Brier's parents had abused all of their kids. Brier's brain damage was a direct result of an episode with his father when he was only an infant. "Go on."

"Anyway, I was telling Jared about me and he got this look on his face. He told me that I was lucky to escape my parents by being put into the hospital. He said he wished he'd been that lucky."

"He was abused as a kid?"

Brier shrugged. "I think so, but he won't really talk about it. I know he can't stand the smell of whisky. He's mentioned that before when we talked about his job. He said sometimes men come into the store and he can smell whisky on their breath and it makes him want to throw up."

Seb knew he had some research to do. "Do you happen to know where Jared grew up?"

Brier nodded. "Broken Arrow, Oklahoma. I remember because I thought it sounded like some place I should've been from."

Seb couldn't help but wonder why Brier thought that. Was it his Native American ancestry or did the man feel he was like a broken arrow? He knew he'd gotten all the information he was likely to get from Brier. From the sound of it, Jared didn't tell his best friend much either.

He stood and held out his hand. "I'll let you two get on the road. Thanks for letting me come over."

Jackie and Brier stood. Jackie gave Brier a kiss on the temple. "Why don't you go into the kitchen and make sure you turned the oven off?"

Brier nodded. "Have a good Thanksgiving, Seb."

"I will. Thanks." Seb knew Jackie wanted to say something to him without Brier being around, so he started to walk towards the door with Jackie at his side.

"What's going on that you aren't telling Brier?" Jackie asked.

"I don't know. I went to invite Jared to dinner at Mac's tomorrow and he got kinda weird about the whole thing. But then again, he was acting strange when I got there." Seb shrugged. "I can't help but think something's going on he's not telling me about."

"Well, if you find out what it is, make sure to give me a call. If there's bad news, I'd rather Brier heard it from me."

Seb smiled. Jackie was so incredibly protective of his partner. Seb had known the man for a number of years and never would have expected him to fall so hard for a lover.

"Have a good weekend." Seb slapped Jackie on the back before retreating to his El Camino. He glanced at the clock and decided to go back to the office for a couple of hours before he had to drive Jared to work.

The bosses had been nice enough to give the entire office staff the afternoon off, but Seb needed to know more about Jared's background. He drove the distance to the office in town that was connected to Mac, Nicco and Amir's home. He parked in front of the redesigned schoolhouse and unlocked the front door.

As he walked down the short hall, he noticed the light in Mac's office was on. "Hey, didn't the boss give you the day off?"

Mac looked up from his computer and grinned. "Nicco and Amir were arguing over the best way to make the stuffing for tomorrow, so I decided to make myself scarce. What're you doing here?"

"Research."

"On?"

Seb knew Mac well enough to know he wouldn't be satisfied until he knew the whole truth. "I need to know about Jared's childhood."

"Why? There are some things that should be left in the past."

Seb thought of his own childhood and couldn't agree more, but this was different. "I need to know why he doesn't want to come over here for Thanksgiving."

Even to his ears, the excuse sounded flimsy. Seb noticed the hurt expression on Mac's face.

"Maybe he's not comfortable with us yet. Or maybe he doesn't like us."

Seb shook his head. "I don't think that's it. It's Thanksgiving he doesn't seem to want any part in. He said he'd think about it, but I could tell he was trying to think up excuses. He asked me something strange though."

"Yeah? What?"

"He wanted to know if people would be drinking."

Mac leant back in his chair and rubbed his neck. "You think his folks were alcoholics?"

Seb nodded. "Brier said something about Jared getting nauseous at the smell of whisky."

"Well, tell Jared we'll be having beer during the game and wine with dinner."

Seb noticed Mac hadn't forbidden him from digging into Jared's past. "I'll find a way to slip that in."

Seb started towards his office, but the sound of Mac's voice stopped him in his tracks.

"If he finds out you dug around in his past, he'll never trust you again."

Seb continued on to his office. As he fired up his computer, he thought about what Mac had said. Was finding out the truth more important than Jared's trust? If he didn't learn the truth, how could he hope to help the younger man, but on the other hand, would Jared even let him help if he found out what Seb had done?

"Shit!" he growled as he shut off his computer.

"I knew you were a better man than that," Mac said from the doorway.

Seb glared at his friend. "You don't have to look so damn smug."

"You like him, huh?"

"What? No. I mean, yeah, I like him, but not the way you're thinking."

"I think you're wrong. I think even if I managed to get Jared another ride to and from work, you'd still insist on doing it yourself."

"No I wouldn't," Seb protested. The last person he'd truly cared about was Alexander and those feelings had nearly killed him. He wouldn't willingly put himself into that position again.

"Fine. I talked to Raven. Since he's the night owl of the group, he's agreed to take over the job as chauffer."

"Raven? Are you nuts? That prick jumps on anything that moves." The thought of Raven being alone at two in the morning with Jared made Seb's skin crawl. It was bad enough that Three Partners specialised in gay bodyguards, but why did they have to employ sluts like Raven?

"He's good at his job and you know it."

"I'm not talking about his job skills, and we *both* know it."

"Does Raven even know who Jared is? Because Jared's still pretty skittish around people he doesn't know."

Mac's grin got even bigger. "He knows Jared, don't you worry about that."

Seb narrowed his eyes at his friend. He knew exactly what Mac was doing. Nope. There was no way Seb was going to bite into that apple. "Fine. I'll tell Jared this evening when I take him to work."

"Yeah, okay." Mac was chuckling as he turned and walked away.

Seb put his feet on top of his desk and leant back in his chair. Raven was known as the shopper because he always got assigned to protect rich men's wives. Like most men, husbands didn't want a straight, good-looking bodyguard following their wives around all day. The perfect solution was hiring a gay man to do the job.

Seb happened to know that didn't stop Raven from getting his groove on though. The man was relentless in his pursuit of cock. As a matter of fact, on more than one occasion, Raven had ended up fucking the husband. The thought of someone like that being with Jared... "Dammit!"

He heard another round of laughter coming from down the hall which pissed him off even more.

* * * *

Jared sat on the couch with his feet tucked under him. The letters continued to taunt him from their hiding place. He kept telling himself nothing good would come from reading them, but he couldn't get them off his mind.

He knew Rick. They were probably filled with hate, or warnings. Jared knew how pissed Rick was when

Brier filed rape charges against him. He knew because Rick took his mood out on him. But Rick was in jail. What could he possibly do to him?

Oh no. What if he was getting out of jail? Maybe Rick was writing to let Jared know?

Jared jumped off the couch, landing as far away from the letters as possible. He knew it was irrational, but he could picture the simple white envelopes staring at him, waiting to reach out and grab him.

He found the broom in the corner of the small kitchen area and turned back to the sofa. He gave the inanimate object a wide berth as he paced back and forth with the broom in his hand. *You can do this.*

Nearing the couch, he stuck the broom under it and snagged one of the letters. He swept the envelope into the centre of the room, well away from the others. Jared took the broom back to its spot in the corner of the kitchen and made himself a glass of ice water.

He sipped at the cold liquid as he circled the waiting envelope. Come on. It's a freaking letter. Don't be such a wimp.

Jared set down his glass and chewed at his fingernail for several moments before reaching down and snatching the letter off the floor. His fingers felt like they were on fire as they tore open the envelope.

As he stared down at the scribbled handwriting, he wished, not for the first time, his reading skills were more advanced. He decided to read what he could and find a way to get hold of a dictionary to help with the rest if he needed.

Pussy Boy,

Jared closed his eyes at the name Rick had always called him. He hated that it still had the power to humiliate him.

I've already told you what I'm plan... to do to you when I get out of here. Well, my brother Bill came to see me today. You rem... Bill, don't you? Even though, like me, Bill's no fag, he sure liked fucking that ass of yours. Bill said he might stop in to say hi. Just tho... you should know.

Rick

Jared took a deep breath as memories of Bill assaulted him. Bill was even meaner than Rick. He was a long-haul trucker who stopped into Lubbock about once a month. It got so bad one time, that Rick actually ordered Bill out of the house.

Jared dropped the letter and retrieved the broom to sweep it back under the couch with the others. What would happen if Bill found him? He looked around his apartment. Never had he been so grateful to be surrounded by strong men.

The longer he thought about it, the more he began to think Rick was bluffing. The last Jared had heard, Rick wasn't even talking to his brother. Besides, Bill worked all the time.

By the time the knock came on the door, Jared had calmed himself down. A quick glance at the clock told him it was Seb. "I'll be right there."

He made sure Jelly Bean had food and water before grabbing his new red coat. "I love you," he told his sleeping cat who was curled up in a chair.

Jared opened the door. "I'm ready."

Seb nodded and led the way towards the elevator without saying anything. Jared wondered if he'd angered him earlier. He knew the Thanksgiving thing seemed to be important to Seb. Maybe Jared should just accept?

He stepped into the elevator beside Seb. "I'll try to come to the dinner."

Seb didn't say anything until they got to the El Camino. Once inside, Seb started up the car and turned the heater on full blast. "What's the real reason you don't want to come?"

"Huh?"

Seb turned to face Jared. "What's your favourite Thanksgiving memory?"

Jared did not want to travel down that road. "I don't have one."

"Why?"

Jared turned away from Seb's intimidating stare and looked out the passenger window. "Just don't."

A loud grunt came from the driver's seat. "I'm not moving this car until you tell me why you don't have at least one good memory of Thanksgiving."

Refusing to be drawn into the discussion, Jared opened his door. "Fine. I'll walk."

With his hands stuffed into the pockets of his coat, Jared stormed off towards town. He heard a car door open and shut and took off running.

"Dammit! Get back here."

Jared shook his head and picked up speed. The blood was pumping so loud in his head, he didn't hear Seb get back into the car. It wasn't until the sleek black El Camino pulled in front of him and slammed on the brakes that Jared realised he was still being followed.

The driver's door opened and Seb flew out of the car straight towards him. It wasn't the first time Jared had been in this position. He did what he'd always done, drop and cover.

Jared didn't know how long he'd been on the ground, but he eventually peeked up around the arms that were covering his head. Seb stood, looking down at Jared with an expression he couldn't read.

Despite Seb's lack of attack, Jared still maintained his position.

"Get up," Seb finally said. "I'm not going to hurt you."

Although the bigger man had said the words, the tone he'd used caused further doubt in Jared's mind.

A strong arm wrapped around Jared's waist and hoisted him to his feet like he weighed nothing.

"Come on, you're gonna be late for work." Seb released him and walked towards the El Camino.

Jared stood rooted to the spot for several moments. Surely if Seb was going to hurt him, he would have already done it. Jared concentrated on putting one foot in front of the other until he was seated in the warm car.

Before pulling away, Seb reached across the distance and put a hand on Jared's thigh. "I'll never hurt you."

Seb removed his hand and put the car into gear. Shame suddenly filled Jared. "I'm sorry."

"If you don't want to go to dinner tomorrow, don't go. I just thought it would be nice having you there."

Jared bit the inside of his cheek. Would his company really make a difference to Seb? "I'll go."

Seb nodded. Within two minutes, Seb pulled in front of the gas station. "I'll be back at two."

"Thanks." Jared felt like he should say more. He knew he'd hurt Seb's feelings, but he wasn't sure how to make it up to him.

"You're welcome."

Jared got out of the car and tried to muster a smile for Seb as he shut the door. Between the letter and questions about his childhood, Jared felt exhausted before he even stepped foot into work. Hopefully the night would go smoothly.

Chapter Three

Parked right in front of the doors, Seb watched Jared as he mopped the shop's floor. He'd yet to get a wink of sleep, throwing his schedule off even further, but his mind had been on Jared. Why that surprised him, was anyone's guess.

The events earlier in the evening still had him shaken. The expression on Jared's face when he'd dropped to the ground was one of trained fear.

Jared spotted him waiting and waved to let him know he would be out soon. Seb acknowledged the gesture as he continued to follow the man with his eyes. What was it that seemed to draw him towards Jared?

Seb gripped the steering wheel. And why did he feel the overwhelming desire to wrap the man in his arms and kiss the life back into him? He knew Jared wasn't the kind of guy who could handle a casual affair, which was the only thing Seb had ever offered a partner, so why did he still keep dreaming about him?

He watched Jared put the money from the cash register into the safe under the counter. Seb knew Jared hadn't locked the door before he did it. He wondered if Jared felt safe knowing Seb was outside waiting or if it was a common practice.

The fluorescent lights over the gas pumps were shut off first, signalling the station was officially closed. It didn't take Jared long to dim the interior lights of the building and lock the front door.

Jared opened the passenger door and climbed in. "Sorry to make you wait. Someone spilled a big slushy in front of the beverage counter."

"That's okay."

The ride back to the dorm was quiet, almost too quiet. Seb wondered if Jared was angry with him, now that he'd had a chance to think things over.

"Would you like a cup of hot tea?" Jared asked as the elevator doors opened onto their floor.

Seb was surprised by the invitation, the first of its kind. "Sure."

He followed Jared into his apartment and was immediately met by Jelly Bean. "Hey there, girl."

Laughing at the way the cat wound herself around Seb's legs, Jared dug into his coat pocket and held up a dented can. "I brought you a treat, Jelly Bean."

Jared gave Seb an apologetic smile. "It was damaged, so my boss said I could buy it for half off."

Seb wondered why Jared felt the need to justify buying a can of food for his cat. "I think you got a good deal."

Jared's smile turned genuine. "I'm not sure if Jelly Bean has ever had the canned stuff. It'll be interesting to see if she likes it."

Jared walked into the corner of the big room and opened the cabinet to get a plate. He pulled the top off the small can and spooned out about a third of it. At the first whiff, Jelly Bean left Seb's side to run into the kitchen area.

"Be patient," Jared scolded his cat as he set the plate on the floor.

Jelly Bean sniffed at the lump of brown goo for several moments before practically inhaling it.

"I think she likes it," Seb chuckled.

"I think you're right," Jared giggled. He filled an old tea kettle with water and set it on the provided hot plate. "Do you want decaffeinated tea?"

"Anything's fine." Seb wasn't normally a tea drinker. It all tasted like hot water with a bit of flavour to him.

Jared got two tea bags out of the box. "My parents were drunks," Jared blurted out without turning around.

"I'm sorry to hear that." Seb moved closer, but not enough to touch.

"You'd never know it by looking at them. Church goers." Jared glanced at Seb and rolled his eyes. "There was a tiny sliding panel in the back of my closet. I'm not sure what the purpose of it was, but when I was little, if I scrunched up real tight, I could fit in there. I can still remember my parents screaming my name as they hunted for me."

The tea pot began to whistle and Jared turned away from Seb to pour the hot water into two mugs. "Believe me. You didn't want to be found when they'd been drinking."

Before he gave himself a chance to rethink his actions, Seb stepped up behind Jared and put his hands on the smaller man's shoulders. "What happened when you were too big for your hiding place?"

"They usually found me," Jared whispered.

How could such a small declaration say so much? Seb leant in and kissed the back of Jared's head. He wondered how far he could push before Jared shut down. Taking a huge chance, Seb released Jared shoulders and reached around the slim body. He ran his fingertips over the scars on one of Jared's wrists. "Is this because of them?"

Jared didn't immediately pull away like Seb half expected him to. Instead he stared down at the scars as Seb continued to smooth over them with his touch.

"I didn't know how else to get away."

"How old were you?"

"The first time? Um, thirteen, I think."

It wasn't until Jared said it that Seb realised there were two sets of slash marks, side by side. "And the second time?"

"Seventeen. That's when the police put me into the hospital."

Seb lifted Jared's wrist and placed a soft kiss on the clean white lines. "Did you ever tell the police the truth?"

"When I was younger. I had an assembly at school that talked about abuse. The film said you should go to an adult like your teacher or a policeman. I went to my teacher. I'm not really sure if she believed me, but she did call the police. They investigated, but like I said, my parents were good at hiding their demons."

Jared shook his head and held up Seb's cup of tea. "You'd better drink this before it gets cold."

Seb could tell Jared was starting to shut down. Seb decided to share a little about his own history. "I was an adult, well, twenty, before I knew what Thanksgiving was supposed to be about."

Jared turned and took a sip of his tea. "Really?"

Seb nodded and took a drink of the god-awful tea. "It's a nice holiday when spent with the right people."

"I know Brier seemed excited about it, but I thought it was because he was going to see his family."

"Yeah, that's part of it. Basically, you lay around watching football until it's time for dinner and then everyone sits down to a big table with more food than they can eat. You talk, you laugh, you finish eating, go back to watching football and then do it all over an hour later with dessert."

Jared yawned. "Sounds nice."

"It is." Seb finished his tea in two swallows and set his cup in the sink. "I'll pick you up at ten-thirty. Will that give you enough time to sleep?"

Jared nodded. "I don't sleep much anyway."

Seb reached out and rubbed his thumb across the dark circles under Jared's eyes. "I know, but try."

"I will. Thanks for coming in."

"Thanks for trusting me enough to invite me." God he wanted to kiss those soft-looking pink lips. Instead, Seb spun on his heels and out the door. Feeling sympathy for the man was one thing, but he couldn't let it become more than that.

* * * *

Jared glanced across the seat to Seb. He had on a pretty black sweater that fit him perfectly. He looked down at his own blue button down shirt. "Are you sure I'm dressed okay?"

Seb smiled. "You look good. It's casual, so you'll fit right in."

"I like your cowboy boots." He wasn't sure what they were made of but some kind of exotic animal no doubt. Jared didn't think he'd ever seen skin like that on a cow.

"Thanks. They're not as comfortable as my regular boots, but I didn't figure I'd be on my feet much today." Seb chuckled. "Actually, I'll probably be sitting on my ass most of the time."

"And you're sure I didn't need to bring anything?"

Seb pointed towards the back of the El Camino. "Hope you don't mind, but I was elected to bring the beer."

"Why would I mind?"

Seb shrugged. "I know you got a little wigged out when I told you there'd be alcohol there."

"I know I did. Sorry about that."

"Don't apologise. It's understandable given what you went through with your folks."

Jared knew it wasn't just his parents' drinking that tainted his views on alcohol, but reminding Seb of the way he'd been abused and kept a virtual prisoner by Rick wasn't something he cared to get into.

Thoughts of Rick brought the letters to mind. He'd gone back and forth with himself since reading them. If he really thought Rick would send Bill to find him, he would tell Seb and the others. Without proof, though, he was afraid of coming off like the pussy boy Rick always accused him of being.

Seb pulled up to the Three Partners' offices, and turned off the engine. "You know, I never asked if you even liked to watch football."

"It's okay. I don't really know the rules, but I can usually figure out what's going on." Jared hoped he could do some work in the kitchen. Groups tended to make him uncomfortable, but then, at least he knew most of the people that would be at the dinner.

It wasn't until he got out and looked in the back of the El Camino that he noticed the two cases of beer. He lifted one, surprised at the weight.

"I can get 'em," Seb offered, lifting the other case easily.

"That's okay. I got it." He repositioned the cardboard box in his hands and followed Seb up the steps to the front door.

Seb balanced the beer on one arm and opened the door. He gestured with his head for Jared to go in.

Once inside, Jared stopped, letting Seb lead the way into the living quarters. He could hear people yelling and started to hang back.

Seb turned and grinned. "They're yelling at the television, not each other."

Jared smiled, feeling stupid. "Good to know."

It was the first time he'd been to Mac, Amir and Nicco's home and couldn't believe the size of the rooms. They entered the living area and sure enough, five guys were sitting on the edge of their seats watching a huge TV screen.

"About time you got here. I thought I'd die of thirst," Raven joked.

Jared didn't really know the man who spoke, but he had met him once or twice in the dorm. He was surprised by the glare Seb shot Raven's way. Jared tried to smooth over the awkward situation by smiling.

"Glad you came, Jared," Nicco called out, momentarily taking his eyes from the television.

"Thanks for inviting me." A few of the other men waved, but their attention was definitely on whatever game they were watching. Jared shuffled from foot to foot, not really sure what to do.

"Come on, Jared, let's put these away," Seb said, nodding to the cases of beer.

Relieved to have something to do, Jared followed Seb into the large open kitchen. He stopped when he spotted Mac grinding his hips against Amir as he kissed him.

"Break it up." Seb chuckled and set his beer on the island.

Although embarrassed at walking in on such an intimate scene, Jared was still unable to take his eyes off the two men who had ignored Seb's order. Had he ever witnessed anything more beautiful than the obvious passion the two men shared for each other?

Seb took the beer out of Jared's arms, breaking his attention away from Amir and Mac.

"You okay?" Seb asked.

Jared wasn't sure he could speak without giving himself away. His gaze went back to the two men. He couldn't stand it, he had to know. "Is that normal?"

"What?"

Jared gestured to the men.

"For them? Yeah. Does it bother you?" Seb asked.

Did it? Jared knew it did but probably not for the reason it would most people.

Seb stepped in front of Jared, blocking his view of Mac and Amir. "Jared?"

Jared gazed up into Seb's dark eyes. There were times when he felt so out of touch. "Is that what it looks like when people really like each other?"

Seb reached out and brushed the back of his hand across Jared's cheek. "Have you ever been kissed because you wanted it?"

Images of Rick forcing his tongue down Jared's throat made him shiver as stomach acid began to churn in his gut. "No, I guess not."

Seb's hand moved to cup the back of Jared's head. As he spoke, his lips got closer and closer to Jared's. "A kiss can be the most sensual touch in the world if done correctly."

Jared felt the heat of Seb's breath caress his lips. He stood mesmerised, wanting to close the distance more than he'd ever wanted anything in his life. *Please. Kiss me.*

"Where's the beer?" Nicco asked, coming into the kitchen.

Seb stopped his forward progress and straightened to an upright position, the moment lost. "On the island. I was getting ready to put it in the cooler."

Still caught in the spell of want, Jared watched Seb turn away. *What just happened?* If it wasn't for the glance Seb gave him over his shoulder, Jared might have thought he'd dreamt the entire moment. He answered Seb's glance the only way he could, with a smile.

Seb returned his smile and began unloading the beer into a large cooler of ice. "Are we gonna leave this in here or take it in the other room?"

"Take it in the other room. The fewer people coming in and out of the kitchen, the better," Mac replied, wiping his mouth.

Jared wanted to offer his help, but the way the three men were looking at each other, he thought they'd prefer he got lost for a while. Resigned to watching football, Jared followed Seb into the main living area. Most of the chairs had already been taken, so he sat on the floor.

With his back against the wall, he watched the group of men yell and scream at the television. Jared didn't understand the point. It wasn't as if the guys playing could hear them, so why do it?

Seb opened the cooler and passed out cans of beer, before finding his own spot to watch the game. Seb sat as far away from Jared as he could get and still see the TV. Jared wondered if the man was regretting the moment they'd shared in the kitchen.

Why wouldn't he regret it? Jared knew he was screwed up. He had absolutely nothing to offer a man like Sebastian. He rubbed his stomach. Something about the near-kiss still had his insides all fluttery.

It was easy to see Seb was nothing like Rick. Jared wondered if it was possible to actually want to do the things Rick had done to him. He was ashamed to admit it, but the few times Seb had touched him in a compassionate way, Jared had actually liked it.

"So I guess I'm going to be your new driver," Raven announced from the chair closest to Jared.

"Huh?"

Raven smiled. Jared knew he'd never seen teeth as white as the Native American's. "Mac asked if I could pick you up from work. Since I'm usually up way past that time anyway, I said yes."

Jared looked at the gorgeous man across the room. Seb met his gaze. Had Seb complained to Mac about picking him up? Jared wouldn't lie to himself, the idea that Seb would do that hurt. He turned back to Raven. "I never asked for a ride. I can walk."

Suddenly the room became claustrophobic. He stood, grabbed his coat off the floor beside him and headed towards the front door. Once outside, Jared sat on the top step. He stared at the bright red coat in his hands but couldn't bring himself to put it on. Had Seb also complained to Mac about Jared not paying him all the money he owed for the clothes?

"Why the hell are you sitting out here in the cold?" Seb asked.

Jared held the coat out. "You should take this back."

"What? Don't be stupid. Put it on." Seb ignored the coat and sat on the step next to Jared.

"I never asked you to pick me up from work. I told you all along I could walk."

"I know you did. But like I told you, it's not safe."

Jared looked up at Seb. "It wasn't the ride I started to enjoy. It was spending the end of my day with you."

Seb broke eye contact and suddenly seemed to find something on the street fascinating. "Guess I enjoyed it too."

Jared snorted. "Yeah, you enjoyed it so much you complained to Mac about it. That's okay. I'm not a charity case. I'll walk."

Seb reached out and touched Jared's hand. "It wasn't like that."

"Whatever." Jared pulled away from Seb's grasp, dropped the coat to the step beside him and stood. "I'm gonna take a walk."

He started down the steps only to be pulled up short when Seb darted in front of him, blocking his path. Seb held the coat in his fist and shook it in Jared's face. "This! Is yours. I may have picked it out, but you bought it. Now put the fucking thing on."

"Is everything okay out here?" Raven asked from somewhere behind Jared.

Freezing his ass off, Jared reluctantly took his coat and did as instructed. Once he had it zipped, Seb grabbed the puffy down in his hands and pulled Jared towards him.

Jared's eyes widened as Seb's mouth closed over his. He opened his mouth to protest when he felt Seb's tongue glide across his own. *Oh.* The soft moan that erupted from Jared's throat was unexpected but not totally unwelcomed.

As if by instinct, Jared's arms wrapped around Seb's neck as the kiss deepened in intensity. Seb's demand gentled and soon the two were trading tongue caresses on the steps of the agency. With Jared standing on the step above, it put their mouths and bodies into almost-perfect alignment.

Want and need threatened to overwhelm him as his hardened cock brushed against the front of Seb's jeans. He felt the strong grip of Seb's hands as they landed on his hips, pulling their lower bodies even closer.

Jared broke the kiss as he struggled to get a breath. What was happening to him? Even not kissing Seb, Jared still felt light-headed. He stared into Seb's eyes, willing himself to ask the questions swirling through his mind. "Why'd you do that?"

Seb opened his mouth before snapping it shut. His eyebrows drew together before separating again. "Because I couldn't not do it." Seb ran his fingers through his hair and stepped away.

A sinking feeling replaced the flutters Jared had earlier. From the expression on Seb's face, he wasn't happy. "So...do you regret it?"

Seb started walking up the steps. He stopped and held out his hand. "Let's go eat."

"But..."

Seb shook his head. "I don't know. Let's just go eat."

Jared reached out to the only man he'd ever wanted. "Will there be pie?"

* * * *

Seb dropped Jared off at work and returned to Mac's. He'd thought about going home to get away from Raven's shitty grin, but knew it would only prompt further snide comments from the asshole.

He wasn't ashamed of kissing Jared in front of Raven, but he was ashamed of the reason behind it. Who the hell did Raven think he was barging in on such an obviously private conversation?

Seb had known in that moment if he didn't stake his claim on Jared, Raven would quickly try to move in. As he pulled Jared into the kiss, he'd told himself it was to protect the smaller man from Raven. At the first swipe of his tongue against Jared's he'd known it wasn't true. He wanted Jared. He'd always wanted him.

Walking through the living room, Seb retreated to the kitchen. He knew Raven and Sal were on clean-up duty and there was something he needed to take care of. "Hey, Sal, can I have a moment alone with Raven?"

The heavily muscled Italian grinned and threw the dish towel at Seb. "As long as you finish up for me."

Seb nodded. "Thanks."

He waited until Sal was out of the room to take the position beside the sink. "Thanks for offering to pick up Jared, but I'll continue doing it."

Raven smiled and handed Seb a plate to dry. "I figured as much."

"It's just that, well, he's not comfortable around most people."

"Mmm hmm, keep telling yourself that," Raven replied, rolling his eyes.

It was obvious Seb wasn't fooling anyone, including himself. "Okay, yeah. I like the guy. There's something about him that brings out my protective instincts."

Raven started to laugh. "You jackass. There was nothing protective about that kiss you laid on him earlier and we both know it. You want to fuck him. You may even actually feel something for him, but don't blame his past for your current feelings."

Seb started to argue but cut his protest short. "Just don't start trying your smooth moves on him, okay?"

Raven shrugged. "Wouldn't do any good anyway. I'll save my moves for the men who can afford them."

"You slut."

Raven chuckled. "Yep, but I'll find a sugar daddy, mark my words. And when I do, I'll be able to give up risking my life to babysit rich society wives."

"Whatever floats your boat." Seb couldn't care less whom Raven let fuck him as long as it wasn't Jared.

He worked with Raven to finish the kitchen. As the evening continued at a snail's pace, he decided to take Jared a plate of leftovers, complete with another big piece of pumpkin pie. Maybe he'd even stick around to keep the man company until he got off work.

Seb couldn't explain his new feelings, but he knew he'd rather spend the evening in a tiny store with Jared than sitting around drinking beer with his buddies.

Chapter Four

With two foil-covered plates on the seat beside him, Seb turned onto the street that would lead him to Jared. As he neared the station, flashing red and blue lights lit up the chilly Thanksgiving evening.

Seb's chest tightened as he pulled as close to the apparent crime scene as he could. He ran towards the gas station and was stopped by a uniformed policeman.

"Sorry, sir, you can't go in there."

Although his heart was racing, Seb knew the guy was just doing his job. "I came to pick up the man who's working. Is he okay?"

The cop gestured to the ambulance. "The techs are checking him out."

"Can I see him?" Seb asked, getting impatient.

The policeman spoke into his radio. "Wait here. The detective would like to talk to you."

"Just tell me if Jared's okay."

"Sorry, sir, I haven't seen him."

Seb began to pace back and forth. He wanted nothing more than to break through the crime scene tape and run to Jared. After everything Jared had been through, Seb couldn't imagine how freaked he must be.

"Sir?" a middle-aged man asked, holding up the bright yellow tape. "Detective Clint Long. Can I speak with you?"

Seb ducked under the tape and started walking towards the ambulance. "If you'll tell me how Jared is."

"He'll be fine. He's bruised, and he suffered a small cut below his right eye. The real problem is he won't talk, so we still don't know what happened here. There was a call placed by that guy over there. He came upon what he thought was a robbery, but if that was the case, the perp sucked at it. As far as we can tell, he didn't even take the money out of the cash drawer."

Seb's training took over. "What did the witness see?"

"A big guy beating up the clerk. But why beat him up if he wasn't after the money? And like I said, your friend isn't talking."

"Did you get a description of the guy?"

The detective shook his head. "Big, white. He was wearing a ski mask, which is why we think it was an attempted robbery."

Seb nodded. "Can I speak to him?"

"Can you get him to talk?"

With everything Jared had gone through, Seb honestly didn't know. "I can try. He's been through a lot. Jared recently pressed charges in Lubbock against a rapist."

Detective Long eyed Seb for several moments before nodding his head. "Do what you can. Our investigation hinges on the information the clerk can give us."

Seb broke away from the detective and jogged towards the ambulance. He knocked on the closed back door and the paramedic opened.

"Yes?"

Seb's gaze zeroed in on the fragile-looking man inside. Although they had several blankets draped over his shoulders, Jared's body was visibly shaking. Seb noticed Jared didn't even glance his way. "Detective Long said I could talk to Jared."

The paramedic nodded. "I put a butterfly bandage on the cut to his head. I think it needs a couple of stitches, but Jared's assured me the bandage will suffice. Other than that, he's bruised. He'll probably be stiff and sore in the morning though."

"Thanks." Seb waited for the paramedic to exit the ambulance before stepping up and in. He ducked his head as he went to sit next to Jared. Finally in the position to do what he'd wanted to do since he dropped Jared at work hours earlier, Seb wrapped the smaller man in his arms.

Jared's body tensed.

"It's okay, babe. I'm here," Seb tried to soothe.

For the first time since he'd arrived, Jared looked at Seb. He collapsed against Seb's side, sinking into the embrace.

Seb kissed the top of Jared's head as the man started to cry. "Shhh, it'll be okay."

Jared shook his head. "No. It won't. Rick won't let it."

Rick? "Jared, what does this have to do with Rick?"

"The police think it was a failed robbery," Jared mumbled.

"But it wasn't?"

Jared shook his head again. "It was Bill."

"Who's Bill?"

"Rick's brother. He warned me. I should've listened." Jared's watery eyes gazed up at Seb. "Why didn't I listen?"

Confused, Seb cupped the back of Jared's neck, keeping him in place. "When did Rick warn you?"

"Letters." Unable to turn his head away, Jared closed his eyes.

"Letters? What letters?"

The ambulance door opened.

"Anything?" the detective asked.

"Jared said it was Bill Sutcliff, the brother of his rapist."

"Do you know this for sure? Did you see his face?"

Jared shook his head, inching even closer to Seb. "I didn't have to see his face to know. His eyes. I've always hated them. It's like he looks at you, but never really sees, ya know? Like there's absolutely nothing behind them." Jared shivered. "I could also tell by the way he hit me. Bill always was a fan of kidney punches."

"He's done this before?" Why wasn't Seb aware of the threat Rick's brother posed Jared.

"Many times." Jared pulled Seb's head down to whisper in his ear. "Rick used to share me with Bill when he was in town."

One thing was certain. Rick wasn't the only one who needed to be brought up on charges of rape and assault.

"Can you arrest him?" Seb asked Long.

"I don't know. I'll take my report back to the station and let my chief and the prosecutor argue it out. Without a positive ID, it might be a tough conviction."

"Can I take him home?"

Clint Long looked over his notes before nodding. "How can I get hold of you?"

"I work for Three Partners Protection. Just call their number and ask for Seb James. Jared doesn't have a phone, but he and I live at the agency's dormitory outside of town. I'll get a message to him if you need me to."

Detective Long turned and said something to one of the policemen. "I'll have Jared's coat brought out. The owner's on his way down to close up the station."

"Tell him Jared won't be back," Seb informed Long.

"I have…"

Seb cut off Jared's protest with a soft kiss. "We'll figure something else out."

He glanced back at the detective. Where he expected to see disgust on the man's face, he saw only acceptance. Whether the guy was gay or not, at least he wasn't a bigot. That moved him up several spots in Seb's book.

Seb felt lips begin to kiss his neck. He knew it was Jared's way of seeking comfort, but he also knew the back of an ambulance wasn't the place for it. "Let's go home, babe."

* * * *

Jared pressed himself against Seb's side once they got in the El Camino. He couldn't explain it, but touching the much bigger man made him feel completely safe. There was something in the way Seb held him that was unlike anything he'd ever experienced. He wondered, not for the first time, what it would be like to make love.

Jared wasn't completely naïve. Even though he'd never experienced love, he knew it was a real thing. Brier had told Jared many times sex was different with someone you cared about.

Taking a chance, Jared reached over and put his hand under the opening of Seb's leather coat. He felt the man's muscles as he slowly ran his hand over Seb's chest. "Thank you for coming to get me."

With his right arm already around Jared, Seb began to rub his side through the big puffy red coat. "I was bringing you over some supper. My heart stopped when I saw the police cars."

At a red light, Jared pulled Seb's head down for a kiss. He opened his mouth and brushed his tongue against Seb's, making the bigger man moan. He couldn't help but smile. He liked that. It made him feel he had some power even though he was so much smaller and weaker than Seb.

The light turned green and a car behind them honked. Seb broke the kiss and continued towards the dorm.

Jared rested his head on Seb's shoulder. He knew he should tell Seb about the letters, but there was plenty of time for that. First he wanted to see if what Brier had told him was really true, plus he wanted to feel that control again. He could think of several ways to make Seb moan.

Seb pulled into the dormitory parking lot and turned off the engine. "Grab that plate beside you. I bet Jelly Bean would love a cold turkey sandwich and mashed potatoes."

Jared removed his hand from Seb's chest and reached to the seat. "What's on the other plate?"

"Pumpkin pie. Bring it too if you feel like eating."

Jared had seen a movie once where the man and woman ate food off each other. He wondered if pumpkin pie would taste better if he licked it off Seb. His cock hardened at the images swirling through his head.

He stacked one plate on top of the other and slid out of the car. Seb wrapped an arm around him as they walked to the front door.

Jared sank further under Seb's protective embrace when they stepped into the building. A group of men, some of them he didn't know, were playing pool in the large common room.

"It's okay." Seb kissed the top of Jared's head. "There's no one here who will hurt you."

Seb pressed the elevator button, shielding Jared from the rest of the room.

As soon as the doors opened, they stepped inside, Seb's back to the closing doors. Jared held the plates to the side and pressed himself against Seb's body. "Can I stay with you tonight?"

Seb ran his hands down Jared's back, more in a comforting caress than a sexual one. "I'd like that."

The doors opened and they exited the elevator. Stopping in front of Jared's door, Seb took the leftovers out of his hands. "You'd better get Jelly Bean. If you don't she'll worry."

Jared hadn't thought of his cat. "Maybe you should just stay at my place. I don't want Jelly Bean to ruin anything."

Seb bent down and kissed him, running his tongue across Jared's lips. "I've got a bigger bed. Besides, a little cat hair never hurt anyone."

Jared was surprised. Rick used to kick Jelly Bean if she got on the furniture. It was one more way the two men were so different. "What about her litter box?"

Seb chuckled. "Unless she's toilet trained, you'd better bring it."

At least Jared had invested in one of the fancy, enclosed boxes. Living in such a small space, he felt it was important. Jared unlocked his door and the fluffy calico immediately came out into the hall to wind her way around Seb's legs.

"Hey, girl, you wanna have a sleepover at my place?" Seb asked the cat.

Seb dug his keys out of his pocket and unlocked his door. "Go on and get what you need. I'll take care of Jelly Bean."

Jared left Seb, trying to coax the cat into his apartment. He took off his coat and hung it in the closet. He was cleaning out the litter box when he thought of the letters again. *Tomorrow.*

He set the litter box and bag of food in the hall as he locked his apartment. The door to Seb's place was shut but not all the way, and Jared carried Jelly Bean's things inside. He wasn't surprised to see his hungry cat already attacking the plate of leftovers.

"Where would you like me to put this?"

"Where do you keep it at your place?" Seb asked, stirring something at the stove.

"Bathroom."

Seb nodded. "Probably be easier to put it in there then."

Jared sited the litter box, then strolled back to the kitchen and interrupted Jelly Bean's dinner to carry her into the bathroom. "See? Just like home."

Jelly Bean looked annoyed and scrambled back into the kitchen to finish her food. Jared picked up the bag of dry food and carried it to the small kitchenette. "What're you making?"

"Hot chocolate." Seb opened a cupboard and handed Jared two bowls. "Do cats drink milk?"

Jared filled one of the bowls with water and set it on the floor out of the way. "They like it, but I don't think it's good for them. Water's fine."

"I've never had a pet. Probably a good thing since I know so little about taking care of them." Seb poured the cocoa into two mugs and rinsed out the pan.

"Pets are easy. All they want is food, water and love." Jared took the offered cup and carried it to the couch.

"Well then, it sounds like pets aren't that different from people." Seb set his hot chocolate on the coffee table and took the mug from Jared's hands. "Let's let those cool for a minute."

Jared flinched as Seb's embrace squeezed against the bruise on his lower back. The action seemed to remind Seb of the earlier events.

"Why was Bill at the station?"

No. No. No. Jared didn't want his night jaded by Rick and Bill. "Can we talk about this in the morning?"

"What about the letters you mentioned? If I'm going to protect you, I have to know the truth about what I'm dealing with."

"Please, Seb. Please let's talk about this later," Jared pleaded.

Seb brushed a kiss across Jared's forehead. "Why don't you want to talk about it now?"

"Because I want you to make love to me," he admitted. It was the first time in his life he'd asked for sex. It started to worry him until he realised it was the first time he'd actually wanted it.

"I'll hold you all night long, but I think you're still too shook up to get into anything as heavy as having sex."

"You don't want to?"

"I didn't say that. I'm sure if my dick could punch me in the mouth it would. But I need to make sure you're doing it for the right reasons. I'll protect you no matter what, but I can't go to the next level without knowing you're ready for it."

Even though Jared knew Seb wouldn't hurt him, he couldn't bring himself to argue back. He knew he was ready. For the first time in his life he was ready. Maybe he could ease Seb into the idea of fucking him.

"Can I still see you naked?"

Seb chuckled. He stood and held out his hand. "You're not going to make this easy for me, are you?"

Jared shook his head. "Do you really want me to?"

Seb led the way across the room, turning off lights as he went. He turned on the small lamp beside the large bed and began to pull the black sweater over his head.

Jared stood mesmerised by the display of sculpted muscles. Seb's body put Jared's to shame. Suddenly, he was sorry he'd asked about getting nude. He studied the intricate tattoo on Seb's chest. It took him several moments to figure out what it said, but when he finally did, he felt sick. He watched as Seb removed the rest of his clothes. Completely nude, Seb put his hands on his hips. "Well, you gonna strip for me?"

"Who's Alexander?" Jared traced the tattoo with his finger. He followed the swirls as they spelled out the name.

Seb reached up and pressed Jared's hand flat against his chest. "He was my brother. But if you can put off talking about the heavy stuff, so can I."

Brother. Knowing it wasn't an old lover helped to put Jared's mind at ease. It was obvious from the expression on Seb's face he didn't want to talk about him. Jared nodded. "Can you turn off the light?"

Seb shook his head. "No hiding that gorgeous body of yours."

"I don't look like you."

Seb reached out and began to unbutton Jared's shirt. Jared turned his head away, unable to witness the disappointment in Seb's eyes once he was finally revealed. Unlike Seb, Jared didn't have tattoos. What he did have were faint scars. The healed wounds were like a journal of his life. He could tell you when and where he got each one of them.

He closed his eyes as Seb's hands began to trace them. "These bruises look pretty nasty. Are you sure you're up for cuddling?"

Jared opened his eyes and looked at Seb. "I know what the paramedic said, but after a lifetime of getting hit, I barely feel it anymore. The bruises will remind me what happened, but they'll be gone in a few weeks."

As Seb continued to explore his chest, Jared reached down and unfastened his jeans. He toed out of his sneakers and pushed his underwear down with the denim. After stepping out of the rest of his clothes, he turned and tried to pull back the covers.

Seb stopped him. He wrapped his arms around Jared's chest from behind and began to explore more of Jared's body. "You're breathtaking."

Jared couldn't hold back a snort. He knew what he looked like and breathtaking definitely wasn't the way he would describe himself.

Seb ignored Jared's non-verbal disagreement and reached down to fondle Jared's balls. "I like the way you feel in my arms. Your skin is so smooth. Makes me wonder what you will feel like to my tongue as I bathe your entire body."

Jared rested his head back against Seb's shoulder. "That's probably the nicest thing anyone's ever said to me."

"Well get used to it. I may be quiet in my everyday life, but I'm a very verbal lover." Seb licked the side of Jared's neck.

Goosebumps broke out on Jared's body at the slight rasp of the goatee against his heated skin. He couldn't wait to touch the bigger man. "Let's go to bed."

Chapter Five

Before getting under the covers, Seb opened the drawer in his small bedside table and tossed a bottle of lube onto the bed. Jared's eyes followed his progress with what seemed to be genuine want. Seb hoped his soon-to-be lover didn't get the wrong idea. "I said I wasn't going to fuck you, but there are other ways to make love."

"Like what?"

Jared lifted the covers, exposing himself to Seb's view. *Damn, the man was sexy.*

"Just relax and feel the moment," he whispered. He kissed the butterfly bandage under Jared's eye, still grateful the man hadn't been hurt worse than he was. Although he'd been fighting his feelings for weeks, Seb knew as soon as he saw the police outside the station, he didn't want to live without him.

For the first time since being separated from Alexander, he yearned to love someone and have them love him back. Maybe it was his age? The older he became, the less he wanted to fuck random men. Images of fucking Jared crept into his mind. God, he wanted to bury his cock as deep as it would go inside the smaller man. One thing Seb's line of work had taught him was that victims of violent crimes often thought they wanted sex when all they really wanted was to feel safe.

Seb refused to allow his relationship with Jared to start off that way. He needed to know for sure the man was in his right mind when Seb truly made love to him for the first time.

He took his time, enjoying the deep, passionate kiss he shared with Jared. Of their own accord, Seb's hands began to wander down Jared's back to cup and squeeze the perfect ass. With a light covering of peach fuzz, Jared's butt fuelled even more fantasies.

Jared broke the kiss and began working his way down Seb's neck before continuing on to his chest. Seb couldn't hold back the groan as Jared's lips surrounded the sensitive, pebbled nub of his nipple.

The farther down Jared travelled, the hornier Seb became. He put his hands on Jared's shoulders, gently coaxing him towards his cock. His hips jerked upward when Jared's teeth scraped through his pubic hair.

"God, that's nice." Seb bent his legs at the knee and spread his thighs as Jared continued southward. "Turn around."

Jared sat up and looked at Seb. "Huh?"

"Let me suck your cock while you suck mine."

Further confusion seemed to settle in Jared's expression. "Why would you do that?"

"Suck you?"

"Yeah."

Seb shrugged. "Because I know it'll make you feel good."

"I've never..."

Seb sat up and pulled Jared into his arms. "No one's ever given you a blow job?"

Jared shook his head.

No longer concerned with his own needs, Seb lay Jared back on the bed. "Let me enlighten you."

Seb started at Jared's nipples, taking first one and then the other into his mouth. He sucked, licked and bit the pale brown discs until they were red and swollen. Seb sat back on his heels and admired the blissful expression on Jared's angelic face. "You like that?"

"Yes."

Satisfied, Seb turned his attention to the long, thin cock that bobbed against Jared's stomach. He repositioned himself until he was on his stomach. He braced his elbows on the mattress and held Jared's bent legs apart. Starting as close to the mattress as he could get, Seb slid his tongue up the crevice of Jared's ass, stopping to circle his lover's puckered hole.

"Oh!" Jared gasped.

Seb promised himself he'd make a feast out of Jared's ass later, but first he intended to give the younger man his first blow job. He knew his skills were rusty, but Jared didn't seem to notice as Seb took as much of the cock into his mouth as he could.

Jared's entire body began to move, writhing in apparent ecstasy as Seb lavished the head with attention. The taste of Jared's pre-cum exploded on Seb's tongue as he lapped up the leaking essence.

Seb felt Jared grab handfuls of his hair as he began a smooth rhythm up and down the length of his lover's erection. He blindly reached for the bottle of lube and slicked his fingers. With his mouth still wrapped around Jared's cock, he began massaging the tight pucker of the gorgeous man's ass.

"I can't. Oh, shit. I can't..."

The first splash of cum on the back of his throat prompted Seb to pull off Jared's length enough to taste the gift he was being given. Jared's body bucked as strings of cum filled Seb's mouth.

It was a first not only for Jared, but Seb as well. Sucking cock had never been all that pleasurable to him. He much preferred to see the eyes of his lovers staring up at him while they sucked his. Not only had he enjoyed giving Jared head, but he knew he'd quickly become addicted to the man's seed.

Above him on the bed, Jared panted, his fingers still wound around strands of Seb's hair.

"Am I dead?" Jared eventually asked.

Seb knew the feeling well. He chuckled as he worked his way up Jared's body to lie beside him. "Feels like it, doesn't it?"

"That was... Oh my God."

Seb cradled Jared against his chest. He felt Jared's hand brush against his cock before wrapping around it. Seb reached down and stilled Jared's hand. "Sleep, babe. There will be plenty of time to play later."

"But you didn't..."

"Shhh, I'm fine." Surprisingly, he was. Had he ever felt satisfied simply by giving a lover pleasure without expecting something in return?

Seb continued to think about it long after Jared had fallen asleep. He wasn't sure what it meant, but he had a sneaking suspicion.

* * * *

Seb sat naked on his bed, surrounded by the letters Rick had sent Jared. He tried to keep his anger aimed at Rick. Although he wished Jared would have shown them to him when he'd received them, he couldn't imagine how scared his lover had been.

"Is this all of them?" he finally asked.

"Yeah."

The letter describing in detail what Rick planned to do to Jared when he got out of jail still had Seb's skin crawling. They were definitely not the writings of a sane man. "We have to give these to Detective Long."

Jared nodded. "I know."

"We should also go down to Lubbock so you can file charges against Bill for rape and assault."

Jared nodded again. He hadn't looked up from petting a sleeping Jelly Bean since he'd handed Seb the letters. "Do you think they'll let me get into my house?"

"Why wouldn't they?"

"Because Rick had the landlord take my name off and put his on instead. After he showed up, he wouldn't let me out of the house. I hadn't been able to get a real job, but I was mowing lawns for people. Rick said I couldn't do that anymore because I might get stupid and tell someone he was living with me."

Seb set the most recent letter down and pulled Jared onto his lap. "Did you ever try to get away?"

Jared nodded. "Once. He found me though. He took me home and tied me up. I was like that for almost a week. He wouldn't feed Jelly Bean. She got so skinny. He said the next time I tried to get away, he'd kill her and make me eat her."

Jared nuzzled his face against Seb's neck. "I tried to get Jelly Bean to run away. I would put her outside after he left the house and pray that she'd run, but she never did. She'd sit at the screen door and meow for me."

"Jelly Bean loves you."

"Yeah. Sometimes I wished she didn't though."

Seb swallowed around the lump in his throat. He knew exactly what Jared was talking about. The tears in Alexander's eyes as he looked out the back window of the social worker's car still haunted him.

Knowing there was nothing he could say to make Jared feel better, Seb continued to hold him in silence. He knew the road ahead wouldn't be easy for either one of them. Not only would Jared have to sit in front of a courtroom and tell what had happened to him at the hands of Rick and Bill, but Seb would have to hear it as well. How would he keep himself from going after the two men with intent to kill?

Seb knew he needed to tell everyone to keep their eyes open for Bill. Until the man was behind bars, Seb didn't plan to let Jared out of his sight. With a building full of trained bodyguards, he knew Three Partners was better equipped than the police at tracking Bill down.

He noticed how quiet Jared had become. He glanced down and realised his lover was asleep. With things to take care of, Seb gently laid Jared on the bed, before covering him up. Before starting on his to-do list, he took several moments to stare at the sleeping man. Even in sleep, Jared didn't look peaceful. The demons that continued to invade his dreams must be stopped.

Seb knew from experience it would take more than sending the two men to prison. Jared would need years of therapy and love to settle him into a peaceful existence. It was a good thing Seb was a patient man where Jared was concerned, because he had a strong feeling things would get worse before they could get better.

* * * *

After taking Jared to the police station to talk to Detective Long, Seb pulled in front of Three Partners. He squeezed Jared's hand. "You understand why we need to ask for their help, right?"

Jared lifted Seb's hand and kissed it. "I understand."

Seb smiled. He wasn't sure if Jared's constant affection was still due to the ordeal he'd suffered the previous evening or if his lover was like a kid with a new toy. It didn't matter to Seb anymore. He didn't plan on complaining a bit.

After years of closing himself off, Seb was enjoying his new-found feelings for the man. He tilted Jared's chin up for a deep kiss. There was something about the consuming way Jared kissed him that made Seb hard every time.

"You ready?"

"Do they know we're coming? What if they're busy?"

Seb laughed. "They know, but that doesn't always mean anything. At any given moment you can pretty much expect at least two of them to be having some form of sex."

"We should definitely call them then."

Seb shook his head and opened his door. "We'll be fine. Come on."

He led Jared up the steps and unlocked the front door. "Hello?"

"Back here," Amir called.

Seb noticed Jared's reluctance. "It'll be fine. Just tell them what you told the detective."

Jared planted his feet and pulled Seb back. "Will you tell them?"

As much as he wanted to make the situation easier for Jared, he knew it wasn't the best thing to do. "The more you tell your story, the easier it will become."

"Okay."

They entered the living room hand in hand. Mac, Nicco and Amir were all tangled together on the big sectional couch. Nicco, who was lying with his head in Mac's lap, reached for the remote and turned off the TV. "Holy Hell. What happened?"

Amir pushed Nicco's feet off his lap and Nicco got into a sitting position. "Have a seat."

Seb led Jared over to the small section of the L-shaped sectional and sat. "There was an incident at the gas station last night."

"What kind of incident?" Mac asked, his eyes narrowing.

Seb knew the look well. Mac was gearing up for a fight with whoever had hurt Jared. He put his hand on Jared's thigh. "Jared?"

Jared twined his fingers through Seb's. "Bill, Rick's brother, paid me a visit. He wore a ski mask, but I know it was him."

"You've met Rick's brother before last night?"

Jared nodded.

Seb could tell his lover was becoming embarrassed, but somehow, he needed to get it through Jared's head that it wasn't something he should be embarrassed by or feel guilty for. He kissed the side of Jared's head. "You can do it."

Jared cleared his throat. "He used to do stuff to me when he was in town to see Rick."

"Stuff? You mean like the stuff Rick did?" Mac questioned.

"Mmm hmm. Sometimes they did it to me together, but most of the time, Rick would go out and leave me alone with Bill. He's married and his wife wouldn't let him do certain things," Jared added.

Seb had been surprised by that nugget of information when Jared told Detective Long. Not only was Bill a rapist, but a cheater as well. For some reason, Seb felt sorry for the man's wife.

"Did the police catch him?" Nicco asked.

Seb decided to give Jared a break. "Not yet. We just left the police station." He glanced down at Jared. "It seems Rick's been sending Jared letters. He told him he'd asked Bill to pay him a visit. We gave the letters to the detective."

"How'd Rick get your address?" Mac sat up further on the couch, resting his forearms on his thighs.

"I don't know. Detective Long said his lawyer might have given it to him off the paperwork I had to fill out when I pressed charges."

"I think we need to check up on Sutcliff's attorney."

Seb nodded. "That's what the detective said as well. I'm taking Jared down to Lubbock to officially press charges down there as well."

"When?" Mac asked.

"This afternoon," Seb informed his boss.

"You need backup?" Amir asked, sitting up straighter.

Seb grinned. He knew Amir missed his days in the field. "Thanks, but I can handle it. We thought you guys might want to inform the men here at the agency and in the dorms to keep their eyes open though."

"You got a picture?"

Seb nodded at Mac and handed him the folded piece of paper from his pocket. "Long pulled that up for us."

"So Bill Sutcliff has a record?" Mac asked, taking the picture before Amir could get to it.

"Yeah, domestic dispute charges, but no convictions." Seb squeezed Jared's hand to make sure his lover was still with him.

Amir whistled when the mug shot was finally passed to him. "Creepy-looking dude."

Seb agreed one hundred percent. Jared had been right on the money when he'd talked about Bill's soulless eyes. With the greasy brown and grey hair and the scruffy beard, Bill looked like he'd be right at home on a street corner panhandling spare change.

Every time Seb thought about the man forcing himself on Jared it made him not only sick to his stomach but mad as hell. "Tell the guys there's no need to go easy on him if they find him lurking around the dorm."

Amir smiled. "I don't think you'll need to worry about that." Amir turned his attention to Jared. "You may have only been here for a short time, but we've all become incredibly fond of you."

"Not too fond, I hope," Seb warned with only a trace of mirth in his voice.

Amir winked. "Some more than others, but fond nonetheless."

Seb rolled his eyes. "Anyway, we're leaving for Lubbock from here. We'll probably spend the night at a hotel and be back sometime tomorrow."

Seb had one more thing he needed to discuss with his friends, but thought it best if he did it without Jared in the room. "Is there any of that turkey or ham left?"

All three men laughed.

"We've got it coming out our ears. Amir's been threatening to make ham salad, turkey salad, turkey soup… Hell, I could go on and on. The man's like that dude from Forest Gump with that shit," Nicco said.

"Would you mind if we fix a couple of sandwiches to eat on the way?" Seb asked.

"Not at all. Help yourself," Nicco told him.

Seb kissed the side of Jared's head. "Would you mind, babe?"

"No. Not at all." Jared stood. "Will you mind if I have to look around for stuff?"

Amir shook his head. "Turkey and ham are in the fridge, of course, bread's on the counter, sandwich bags in the middle drawer on the left side of the island."

After Jared left to fix their lunch, Seb addressed his friends. "I hate to ask, but I was wondering if the agency has any available jobs Jared could do? I don't like the idea of him working at that gas station anymore."

"Don't blame you," Mac said. "But I think the only thing we're advertising for is custodial help for the dorms. I don't know how Jared would feel about that."

"Nothing wrong with custodial work. I'm sure he'd be thrilled, plus it would solve our transportation issue."

Mac rubbed his jaw. "Tell you what. You tell Jared we'll pay him two hundred and fifty bucks a week plus rent. We'll even throw in cable television."

"What're his hours?" Seb asked.

"Days, Monday thru Friday, ten to five, an hour for lunch."

Seb grinned at Mac. "Pretty cushy hours."

Mac shrugged. "Can't vacuum too early in the morning or I'll have some pissed off guys. Those hours should be more than adequate to get the job done. I'll send a list of duties along with the employment paperwork out to the dorm with Amir on Monday morning."

"Sounds good. Thanks."

Mac waved his hand. "It's a job that needs doing, and I feel better about giving it to someone I already know."

Jared came back into the room carrying four sandwiches. "I hope this is okay."

Nicco chuckled. "Okay? You've just saved me a day's worth of turkey gumbo."

Amir gave the back of Nicco's head a playful slap. "You like my gumbo, so shut up."

"Yeah, for one meal. No one wants to eat leftovers for an entire week," Nicco argued.

"Fine. You figure out what to do with them," Amir countered.

Seb decided it was a good time to leave. The three men often argued just so they could make up, and he didn't think Jared was ready to witness either of them. "You ready?"

Jared's gaze went from Amir and Nicco to Seb. "Yeah."

Seb stood. "I'll see you Monday, Mac."

Mac smiled and nodded. He also knew what was coming and it didn't appear he minded one bit.

Seb led Jared out of the building and to the El Camino. "Don't pay them any mind. It's a game to them."

"A game?" Jared asked, getting in the car.

"Argue and then make up."

"Oh."

Jared still had a confused expression on his face. Seb continually forgot Jared hadn't been exposed to normal relationships. He pulled away from the kerb and headed out of town. "When two people, or in their case, three people are together all the time, it's normal to have occasional disagreements. The difference is that when you really care about the person you're arguing with, it's natural to then eventually make up."

Seb glanced at Jared and winked. "Usually the making up involves time in bed making love."

"Oh," Jared said like he understood. "So Nicco and Amir weren't really mad at each other?"

Seb shook his head. "Naw. They're all probably making up as we speak."

Jared grinned and rubbed his hand across Seb's thigh. "That making up thing sounds like fun."

Seb bit the inside of his cheek as Jared's hand roamed higher on his leg. He'd made the decision in the wee hours of the morning to hold off fucking Jared until the ordeal with Rick and Bill was over.

Once Jared knew he was no longer in danger from the two men, he would be better equipped to make the decision on whether or not to take their relationship to that next level. Seb just hoped he could hold off that long. There wasn't a minute of the day he didn't think about driving his cock deep into the younger man's ass.

When Jared's hand began groping Seb's cock through the tight material of his jeans, Seb knew he'd have to put a stop to it. He reached down and moved Jared's hand back to his leg. "It's hard enough to concentrate on the road with you sitting so close to me. Keep that up and I'll drive us into the ditch."

"Sorry." Even though Jared said the words, Seb caught the grin on his lover's lips.

* * * *

The closer they got to Lubbock, the more uneasy Jared started to feel. He knew he needed to get his mind off his old life with Rick and Bill, or he'd completely psych himself out. Since playing with Seb wasn't an option, he decided it might be the perfect time to get the bigger man to open up about his past.

"You still haven't told me about Alexander. Do you still keep in touch with him?"

The car swerved a little before Seb righted it again. "He's dead."

Jared held his breath, afraid he'd upset Seb. He should have never brought it up. He looked out the passenger window, but began rubbing his hand in soothing circles on Seb's thigh.

Seb didn't say anymore, but he did thread his fingers through Jared's. They rode in silence for several miles before Seb finally spoke. "Mac said to ask you if you'd be interested in the custodial job at the dormitory? He said he'd pay you two hundred and fifty a week plus rent."

A thousand dollars a month, plus rent? Jared was immediately suspicious of the offer. "Did you ask him to give me a job?"

Seb shrugged. "I asked if he had anything available." Seb glanced at Jared. "Mac's a businessman. Believe me, he wouldn't hire you if he didn't have the work."

"But a thousand dollars? Why do I need that kind of money?" Jared had never in his life even seen that much money. No way would he ever have dreamt he could make that much in just one month, especially since he didn't have to pay rent.

"Don't forget the government will take a good chunk of it. You should save some of it. Maybe someday you'd like to buy a car or have new clothes," Seb suggested.

"Or a house!" Jared got so excited he clapped his hands together. "One that wasn't a rental, so I could paint the walls."

"You don't like the dorm?" Seb asked.

"Sure, I like it, but everyone has to have a dream, right?"

"And yours is to buy a house?"

Jared nodded. "It may sound silly to you, but I've always dreamed of living in a peaceful place. A space where I don't have to hear people yelling at me. A place where I can feel safe."

Seb reached for Jared's hand and brought it to his lips for a kiss. "That doesn't sound silly at all. I hope you get it."

"What about you? Have you ever wanted a house?"

Seb shook his head. "I've moved around a lot, so it's better not to get too attached to one place."

"Oh." Jared's stomach started churning. Did Seb's statement include getting attached to people, too? Maybe he was being naïve, but he thought he and Seb were really starting to connect. He'd even hoped that someday they might share a house. *Stupid.* That's what he got for thinking too much.

* * * *

By the time they finished at the police station, Jared was wrecked, but at least a few things had been cleared up. According to the police, Bill had visited his brother in jail on several occasions. The detective they spoke to guessed Bill took the letters from Rick and mailed them to Jared.

Although Seb hated that Jared had received them in the first place, at least there was something substantial to tie Bill's actions to Rick. Thankfully they'd given the letters and envelopes to Detective Long earlier that morning. The detective in Lubbock said he'd get with Long about fingerprinting the pieces of paper.

With Jared glued to his side, Seb stopped at a stop sign and kissed the top of his lover's head. "You sure you feel up to going by your old place? We can always call it a day and do it in the morning."

Jared shook his head. "I don't want to stay here tonight. If I had my way, I'd never come back, but I know that's not going to happen."

After what Jared had just gone through, Seb hated the idea of the younger man testifying in front of a roomful of people. Now he knew why Jackie and Bram were so worried about Brier testifying. Not only would Jared have to suffer through the two trials in Texas, but most likely they would then transfer Rick to Oklahoma where he'd stand trial for the rapes he committed at the psychiatric hospital where he'd met Brier and Jared.

"Do you have a key to the house?" Seb asked.

"No, but I know where Rick hid one for Bill to use."

Against his better judgement, Seb followed Jared's directions to the house. When he pulled into the drive, he wanted to break down in tears. He'd never seen a more depressing place in his life. Even his mother, the drug whore, had lived in a better place.

The entire paint-bare house leant towards the side like it could topple over at any minute. He glanced at Jared and noticed the man was looking straight at him, no doubt, to see his reaction to the place. "You ready to do this?"

Jared nodded. "The rent was cheap. When I got out of the hospital, no one wanted to hire me. I managed to get into this place by going to one of the local churches for help. It sucked, but it was mine, at least for a while."

Until Rick moved in. He turned and wrapped his arms around Jared. "If it gets to be too much, tell me."

"I will." Jared tilted his chin up, obviously in need of a kiss.

Seb had no problem fulfilling that need for his lover. He put all his compassion and feelings into each swipe of his tongue, hoping it would be enough to settle the younger man.

Pulling back, he rubbed his nose across Jared's. "Let's get this done and get the hell out of town."

"Good idea."

They exited the car and Jared gestured to the porch. "Have a seat. I'll go find the key. Last time I saw it, Rick hid it in the shed out back."

"Want me to help you look?" Seb asked.

"No. I'll get. You might make sure someone else hasn't already moved in though." Jared walked around the side of the house.

Seb stood on the decaying porch for several minutes before deciding to knock on the front door. With every wrap of his knuckles, he thought the fucking thing would fall off its hinges.

Satisfied the place was empty, he sat on one of the cement steps leading up to the porch. He heard clattering behind the house and then silence. He figured Jared must've finally found what he was looking for.

After several more minutes and still no sign of Jared, Seb stood and wandered around the side of the house. The shed door, if you could even call the dilapidated building a shed, stood wide open. "Jared?"

When he received no answer, Seb stepped foot inside the dank smelling building. His stomach sank when he realised the shed was empty. He turned and rushed back outside. "Jared!"

Seb studied his surroundings. He knew Jared wouldn't have left on his own. He raced to the alley behind the shed and looked both ways. Not a car in sight. He tried to think back. Had he heard a car start? *Fuck*. The neighbourhood was fairly typical with cars driving by, he probably wouldn't have even given a starting car a second thought.

Seb ran down the one-way alley to one of the paved streets. "Jared!"

Knowing the police could help him canvass more area that he could alone, Seb hurried back to the El Camino. He grabbed his phone out of the glove compartment and dialled 9-1-1.

Seb knew he'd never forgive himself for failing to protect the one person on earth he loved. He swallowed around the lump in his throat. Why had it taken his lover's disappearance to realise the full extent of his feelings for Jared?

Seb shook his head as the operator came on the line. There would be plenty of time to punish himself. His number one priority was to find Jared.

Chapter Six

Jared was searching the empty flowerpots for the key, when he felt a presence behind him. At first he thought it was Seb until a hand covered his mouth at the same time a knife blade was held against his throat.

"Make one sound, and I'll kill you right here," Bill growled in Jared's ear.

He had no doubt Bill would do it. Slipping back into his past, Jared allowed himself to be turned and pushed out of the shed. He felt the point of the knife dig into the skin of his back with every step.

In the alley, two houses down, sat Bill's old, rusted car. Jared wondered where Bill planned to take him.

"Stop," Bill ordered. He unlocked the trunk and gave Jared a shove. "Get in."

Like he always had, Jared did what he was told, afraid of the repercussions if he didn't follow orders. The trunk was completely empty, not even a blanket to cushion his body, as he was shut inside the cold, dark place.

Jared remembered the small space he used to squeeze into when he was a child. He wrapped his arms around his legs and pulled them to his chest. As the car pulled out, Jared's head smacked against the hard metal underneath, the smell of the exhaust slowly seeping into the confined space. Maybe he'd get lucky and die of carbon monoxide poisoning before Bill had a chance to hurt him again.

* * * *

Seb rubbed his eyes. He'd spent the last seven hours driving the streets of Lubbock and the surrounding communities, hoping to spot Bill's blue, 1978 Ford Fairmont. He was lucky the police had not only given him a description of the car but the licence plate number as well.

The phone beside him rang and he grabbed it up, hoping for word. The caller ID dashed his hopes. "Hey."

"Anything?" Mac asked.

"No. You?"

"Not yet. Why don't you come back to the hotel and we can organise the men."

"I can't. I can't stop until I find him." Commotion in the background got Seb's attention. "What's going on?"

Mac didn't answer right away. Seb could here snippets of conversation between Amir and Nicco, but not enough to know what the hell was going on. He definitely heard Bill's name mentioned.

"Mac! What the fuck's happening?" he asked, exasperated.

"They found Sutcliff's car at a truck stop outside of Santa Rosa, New Mexico. That puts him over the state line, straight into federal jurisdiction."

Why would he take Jared back to New Mexico? Seb knew there was something he was missing. "Do we have anyone investigating Bill's past? There's got to be a reason he'd transport Jared over state lines instead of just kill…"

Seb swerved to the side of the road. He opened his door and threw up what little he had in his stomach. For hours he'd fought himself to remain positive. He couldn't let thoughts of what Bill might do to Jared deter him from the task at hand. The important thing was to keep looking until he found the man he loved.

He wiped his mouth with the back of his hand and sat up. "I'm on my way to Santa Rosa."

"Wait right where you are. There's no sense in all of us driving separately. I'll send someone by to pick you up. Maybe you can get a few hours of sleep on the drive. You're not going to be much good to us if you're asleep on your feet," Mac informed him.

Seb gave Mac directions to the nearest strip mall. "I'll wait ten minutes. If someone's not here, I'm leaving."

Seb shoved his phone into his jacket pocket. He reached across the seat and opened the glove box, grabbing his Glock before driving the short distance to the shopping centre. After parking under a security light, he got out and dug out his shoulder holster from behind the seat.

He tore off his jacket and fit the holster into place before slipping the black Glock into place. Seb shrugged back into the jacket, concealing his weapon. He locked up the El Camino and waited for his ride.

As he paced the area beside the car, he realised he hadn't received an answer to his question about Bill's past. Surely Mac had someone digging into it.

A non-descript sedan pulled up and Seb got in. He was only a little surprised to see Archer Adams behind the wheel. "Aren't you supposed to be on tour with Keifer?"

Archer shook his head. "Keifer decided to cancel his next few gigs. He felt he needed some time back with his family in Des Moines."

"And you didn't follow him?" Seb asked as Archer tore out of the parking lot.

"He didn't want me there. Besides, without those god-awful clothes, hair and makeup, he doesn't look like a rock star at all. He assured me most people from his hometown don't even know Jimmy Cook is Keifer Zane."

Seb put the seat back and the backrest down until he was in a comfortable position. He didn't know if he could sleep, but he knew Mac was right about him getting some rest. It was after midnight and he was hours away from Santa Rosa.

"So this kid means something to you?" Archer asked.

"His name's Jared. And yes, he means everything to me." There. He'd finally admitted his feelings out loud. Seb hated himself for telling Archer before he'd even had a chance to tell Jared. He'd been a stubborn sonofabitch, refusing to come to terms with how he felt. That would all change when he found his lover. Seb planned to spend the rest of his life making sure Jared was not only safe, but his number one priority.

"You know this isn't an easy line of work to be in and hold a relationship together," Archer commented.

Seb knew Archer was speaking from experience. Since Archer's break-up from fellow bodyguard Joe Rinehart, the man seemed to have sworn off men all together.

"I know, but Jared means more than a damn job. I'll quit if I have to."

Archer whistled. "Never thought I'd hear those words come out of your mouth, boss."

"Never thought I'd be in the position to say them."

Archer reached over and gave Seb's thigh a thump. "Get some sleep. I'll get you to Santa Rosa."

* * * *

By the time Jared felt the car stop, he'd already thrown up twice. He'd searched in vain for something, anything to defend himself with, but Bill had done a good job of cleaning out the space.

When the trunk opened, Jared wasn't surprised to find it had gotten dark outside. Staring up at the face of his kidnapper, Jared prayed Bill would kill him quick.

"Wake up, pussy boy," Bill cackled.

Bill grabbed the front of Jared's red coat and pulled him out of the trunk. Jared had to blink several times before he believed what he saw. He was surrounded by dilapidated trucks and trailers in what seemed to be some kind of junk yard.

Before he could ask, the knife was once again against his throat as Bill marched him towards one of the trailers, half sunk into the ground. Was that to be his grave? Where was Seb? Was anyone even searching for him?

"Here we go. Home sweet home," Bill said, opening the back door of the semi trailer.

Bill pulled a lighter out of his pocket and lit a kerosene lamp just inside the door. As soon as Jared saw the cage, he knew. It was the same cage Rick had used to train him when he'd first moved himself in with Jared.

"No!" Jared began swinging his arms, no longer caring if Bill slit his throat. He'd rather die than go back in there.

He felt the satisfying crunch of Bill's nose as his flailing fist connected.

"You son-of-a-bitch!" Bill howled, grabbing Jared by the hair and slamming his head into the side of the trailer.

Jared's legs gave way and he slumped to the floor. In a fit of pure rage, Bill began kicking Jared across the trailer towards the cage. Jared tried to wipe the blood that ran into his eyes as he moved to get away from the punishing kicks.

"Goddamn my brother. I wanted to just fuck ya and kill ya but noooo, he insisted you be made to suffer like he's suffering."

In the end, Jared crawled into the cage to get away from the constant pain of Bill's steel-toed boots. Bill aimed one last kick at Jared's ass before slamming and padlocking the door. Jared curled himself into a protective ball as Bill continued to hurl obscenities at him.

Bill eventually seemed to calm down and the trailer quieted. Jared flinched as he heard Bill's zipper lowering. *No. Please. No.*

Jared squeezed his eyes shut and waited for the cage door to open once again. He swallowed the bile rising in his throat as he heard the all too familiar sound of Bill jacking off. Christ, the fucker was getting off on seeing Jared in the cage. He remembered Bill and Rick both standing over his cage doing the same thing on many occasions.

Bill let out a loud grunt as warmth splashed across the hand Jared was using to shield his head. More strings landed in his hair, and Jared lost the battle. He scooted as close to the back of the cage as he could and vomited.

"Oh, fuck. That's nasty," Bill growled, kicking the cage.

Jared didn't dare wipe his mouth or the blood from the fresh cut on his head, instead choosing to keep himself shielded as much as possible from Bill's wrath. He heard Bill's zipper slide back into place and breathed a sigh of relief.

"I gotta go ditch the car, but I'll be back, pussy boy. I'm not near done with you yet."

The light was extinguished and the trailer door shut, leaving Jared alone in the dark. He wiped his mouth on the front of his shirt and reached up to feel his forehead. The cut was only about an inch long. Jared was confident it wasn't life-threatening, although he was starting to wish it were.

The cage wasn't tall enough to allow him to sit up, so he remained where he was. *Think.* He reached out and ran his hand over the familiar grid-pattern of the dog crate. Frustrated, he kicked his feet against the wire mesh.

Jared stilled. Did he feel a little give in the wall or was it his imagination? He kicked out again, wishing the cage was big enough to use the full force of his legs. Yes.

Jared manoeuvred himself as far against the opposite side as he could get, giving his legs a little more room, and kicked again. He felt the contact rattle his bones and travel up to his aching head, but he was now positive he could eventually free himself.

If he was going to die, it wouldn't be in the fucking cage.

* * * *

Jared knew his time was running out. It had taken all his strength to kick his way out of the cage. In the end, he'd managed to open a large enough area to squeeze through. He was grateful for his jacket. Although the puffy down had made it a tight fit, the coat protected his skin from the sharp, broken wires.

He sat with his back against the wall, trying to figure out what to do next. He couldn't get the images of Seb finding his dead body out of his mind. Jared hadn't said it, but he thought he might be in love with Seb. He remembered how closed-off Seb was when they'd first met. Jared hadn't managed to completely break down the man's walls, but he would get there, even if it took him the rest of his life.

The thought reminded him that he may never see Seb again. What if he died? Besides Seb and Brier, would anyone else care? Although he'd managed to get out of the cage, the trailer door was locked, trapping him once again. It seemed to be the way of things for him. Every time he managed to escape one horrible situation another seemed to find him.

No. He may have laid down and took it in the past, but he had something to fight for now. He had Seb, and Jared knew he'd fight to the death for one more kiss from the man. There had to be something he could use as a weapon. He began crawling around the dark floor of the trailer, wincing as a sliver of wood pierced the skin of his palm.

He sat back down and blindly tried to remove the splinter, wishing he had some light. *Light! The lamp.* Jared felt along the wall until his hand bumped the lamp.

He could hear the fuel in the base of the lamp but he wasn't sure how to get at it. Jared began twisting and pulling the various pieces until he'd almost completely disassembled the thing. The smell of kerosene almost overwhelmed him in the enclosed space, but he knew he needed to be ready. If he was lucky, he'd get one chance at it.

As he sat in the dark, hoping Bill would return, Jared realised that for the first time in his life he wanted to live. He ran his fingers over the thin scars on his wrist. Twice he'd tried to end his pain and he'd failed. Maybe if he'd known someone like Seb, things would have been different. Maybe he wouldn't have let himself be tortured and kept prisoner by Rick when he'd caught up with him in Lubbock.

Jared knew hanging his hopes of a future on one man wasn't the smart thing to do, but just knowing there was more out there than what he'd grown up with was enough.

The time seemed to creep by until he heard it, the rumble of a semi pulling up next to the trailer. Jared got to his feet and stood against the wall. He poised the open lamp at approximately the right height and held his breath as the padlock was released on the door.

The door swung open and right on cue, Bill flicked the lighter to life. "I'm home..." That was as far as Bill got before Jared doused the front of his tormenter with kerosene. A ball of fire erupted as Bill screamed, trying to knock the fire from his face and chest.

Jared kicked out with all his strength and Bill toppled to the ground. Jared ran out of the trailer and aimed the rest of the fuel at Bill's rolling, burning body. He dropped the lamp to the ground and ran to Bill's truck. He struggled to breathe as he climbed into the cab and locked the doors.

With no keys, Jared knew he couldn't go anywhere, but at least he was safe. He reached for the CB radio and turned it on. "Hello? Please, can someone help me?"

* * * *

Seb's phone woke him about an hour after he'd drifted off. "Yeah."

"They've found Jared," informed him. "At a junk yard outside Plainview, Texas."

Seb swallowed around the lump in his throat. "Is he…?"

"They think he's okay. He called from Bill's semi. The police are on their way."

Seb looked at Archer. "Turn around. They've found Jared outside Plainview."

"We just passed it about twenty minutes ago," Archer said, checking traffic before cutting across the median to head in the opposite direction.

"Give me directions to the junk yard." Seb relayed them to Archer as Amir rattled them off. "We should be there in about ten minutes."

Archer got the hint and stomped on the gas.

Seb rocked back and forth in his seat, anxious to make sure for himself that Jared was okay.

"What about Sutcliff?" Archer asked.

"I don't know. Right now, I don't care. All I want is to see Jared."

Archer nodded, his eyes still on the road. "We'll get you there."

After several hair-raising turns, Archer pulled the car into the junk yard, the area illuminated by the headlights of around six police cars. Seb jumped out and ran towards the gathered policemen. "Where is he?"

One of the uniformed officers pointed to the semi. "He won't come out."

"Yeah he will." Seb ran to the truck and stepped up on the running board. Jared sat, staring straight ahead, dried blood covering the side of his face. Seb's chest squeezed at the blank expression on his lover's face.

"Jared?" he yelled through the glass. "Jared, baby? Are you okay?"

Jared blinked several times before turning to look out the window. It seemed to take a few moments before Seb's presence registered. He reached out and unlocked the truck door.

Seb stepped down, opened the door and pulled a dazed Jared into his arms. Neither of them spoke. Seb didn't know that he'd ever held anyone tighter or with more feeling. He knew he couldn't let another moment slip by without telling the man just what he meant to him.

"I love you," he whispered into Jared's ear.

Jared started to sag towards the ground. "I love you, too."

Seb easily lifted the man into his arms and looked around for somewhere warm to take his lover. Jared wrapped his arms around Seb's neck and held on.

Seb passed the cops, still gathered in a clump outside a trailer. "Have you called an ambulance?"

One of the policemen nodded. "This guy's obviously dead. How's he doing?" he asked, gesturing to Jared.

"I haven't had a chance to check yet. I'm going to take him to the car until the paramedics arrive." Seb noticed the charred body on the ground. He couldn't believe he hadn't recognised the smell in the air earlier.

"I did that," Jared said, gazing up at Seb.

"It's okay, babe."

Jared's focus went to Bill's body. "I did that. I can't believe I did that."

The policeman stepped towards them. "Is he ready to give his statement?"

Seb shook his head. "Let's wait until he's checked out. Looks like he's taken a pretty good hit to the head."

"I'm not crazy," Jared said.

"I know you're not. I just think you need a little time before you start answering questions." Seb turned away from the policeman and carried Jared towards the sedan.

Archer was waiting for them and opened the back passenger door as they neared. "How is he?"

Seb nodded. He still couldn't get the picture of the burned body out of his mind. Right or wrong, he wanted to know where Jared's courage had come from. Seb figured few people who'd been through the things Jared had, would be able to not only stand against their attacker but kill them in the process.

Seb laid Jared on the seat and ran around to the other side of the car. He got in and rested Jared's head on his lap. "What happened to your head, babe?"

The corner of Jared's mouth tilted up just a fraction. "I punched him in the nose and then he ran my head into the side of the trailer." Jared actually smiled. "It was worth it."

Seb shook his head. "You absolutely amaze me." He leant down and gave Jared a deep, but short, kiss.

The ambulance pulled into the junk yard followed by several more police cars and sedans Seb knew were carrying Three Partners employees. "We're gonna get you all checked out, okay?"

Jared nodded. "Then will you take me home?"

"I will as soon as I can, but you need to talk to the police first."

Jared averted his eyes and shook his head. "I don't want to go to jail." He looked up at Seb, tears filling his eyes. "He put me in a cage."

One of the paramedics started to open Seb's door, but he pulled it shut again and held his hand up to the man, silently asking for a moment. He pulled Jared into his lap. "Sweetheart, I don't know what went on today, but I do know none of it was your fault. There's no way in hell you're going to jail."

"When you told me you loved me, it was before you saw what I did to Bill. Do you…"

"Yes, I still love you." Seb hugged Jared, placing a kiss beside the fresh cut on his forehead. "I know this might not be the time to tell you this, but I'm so incredibly proud of the way you held yourself together during all this. I'm in awe of your strength and your heart."

Jared wiped at the tears rolling down his cheeks. "I just suddenly knew I wanted to live, because for the first time in my life, I have something to live *for*."

The paramedic knocked on the window, looking pissed.

"Let's get you looked at, take care of the police and then we can go home and love on Jelly Bean."

Jared nodded, his throat working as if he was trying to swallow his tears.

Seb opened the door and helped Jared from the car and into the care of the paramedics. He walked over to Amir, Mac, Nicco and Archer who were standing to the side, watching the crime scene techs take pictures.

"What's going on? Why all the pictures?" he asked the group.

"I think they're just trying to gather evidence to strengthen the case against Rick. If Bill did act on Rick's orders, they'll try to find the connection," Mac told him.

There were large spotlights set up in and around the trailer. Seb's gaze zeroed in on the broken and twisted cage. Jared's words came back to him. He tried to imagine his lover, scared, locked in the cage. Seb felt something he'd rarely experienced. He turned away from his friends and walked into the shadows, wiping the moisture from his eyes.

Seb wasn't sure how long he stood in the dark, wondering how he could ever be strong enough to help Jared through an ordeal like he'd just been through. Being kidnapped, stuffed into a dog crate and then actually setting a man on fire? How could an already emotionally damaged person crawl out of the depths Jared must've been taken to?

Memories of Alexander assaulted him. He'd been unable to save his baby brother, but he'd been a boy himself. Seb took a deep breath. He was no longer a child, and he knew he'd do everything in his power to pull Jared out of those depths and show him that he deserved to live a life of happiness and love.

A hand landed on his shoulder. Seb turned around and was surprised to see a bandaged Jared standing in front of him. "Did the paramedics get you all fixed up?"

"Yeah." Jared gestured to his forehead. "Another butterfly bandage, a couple of bruises and some pretty deep scratches on my lower legs, but nothing I can't take care of at home. Will you go with me to talk to the detective? I don't think I want to go through it more than once, and I know you deserve to know what happened."

Seb held out his hand and smiled. "From now on, wherever you go, I go."

Chapter Seven

Jared didn't even remember getting home, but when he woke, he was snuggled against Seb's chest with Jelly Bean curled around his feet. He opened his eyes and smiled at the small lamp across the room Seb had obviously left on for him.

He didn't know how long it would take to get the images of Bill's burned body out of his mind, but he didn't feel guilty about what he'd done. Even after talking to the police, he felt no remorse.

By the time they'd finished at the police station in Lubbock, he and Seb were both dead on their feet. Jared had suggested they find a hotel and sleep, but Seb had insisted he get Jared home to Jelly Bean.

In the end, they'd both slept in the back of Archer's rented sedan for the four hour drive home. Evidently, Seb had carried him into the building and put him to bed. Jared wasn't sure if it was the stress of the previous day or the pain pill Archer had given him to combat the almost-debilitating headache he'd had after the police interview.

Jared turned his head to kiss Seb's chest. It had taken several minutes of convincing before Seb had agreed that one pill wouldn't do him harm. Just like he'd promised, Seb had been by his side the entire time. Jared could tell how much it had cost Seb to keep his temper in check as Jared described in detail what had happened.

Jared managed to scoot back far enough to study Seb's gorgeous face. He still didn't understand why such a strong, handsome man had fallen in love with him. It was obvious Seb could have any guy he wanted, he hadn't missed the covert glances Archer aimed Seb's way. *So why me?*

Still asleep, Seb reached out and pulled Jared back into his arms.

Jared let the man have his way. He knew there would be plenty of time to ogle his lover in the future. The future? *Wow. I actually feel like I have a future now.* He couldn't help but smile.

Movement at his feet told him Jelly Bean was up. Jared didn't even have to look at the clock to know it was near noon. If there was one thing that had been a constant in his life with the sweet cat, it was her feeding routine and twelve was lunch.

When he didn't immediately get up, Jelly Bean walked up the length of his body and started kneading his side. Jared flinched as the cat managed to touch one of the fresh bruises left by Bill's boot.

Seb's arms tightened. "What's wrong?"

"Jelly Bean says it's time to eat." Jared leaned back on his elbow and stared up at his lover. "You keep the bed warm, and I'll pour her some food."

"I'll do it," Seb said as he slid his arm out from under Jared.

"No you won't. You go back to sleep." Jared leaned down and playfully bit Seb's nipple, following it up with a leisurely lick.

Seb moaned and pulled Jared into a kiss, thrusting his tongue deep. Jared let his hand wander down the length of Seb's chest to his lover's hardening cock.

Seb broke the kiss and smiled. "I'm definitely up now."

Jelly Bean chose that moment to pounce on Seb's stomach, eliciting a grunt from the big strong bodyguard.

Jared chuckled. "She won't be put off. Believe me."

He gave the heavily veined erection one last squeeze before releasing it and moving towards the side of the bed. "This won't take long. Promise."

Seb rolled over and propped his head up on his hand. "Would you please bring me a bottle of water out of the fridge when you come back?"

Jared nodded and replaced the covers, hoping it would keep his side of the bed warm until he returned. Naked, he walked across the room and poured Jelly Bean's dry food into a bowl. He could feel Seb's eyes on him as he moved about the small kitchenette.

Only a short time ago, the attention would have mortified him. With Seb it was different. Seb didn't appear to be disgusted with the bruises. Jared knew they bothered him, but not for the reason he used to think.

Jared grinned to himself and put an extra sway in his step on the way back to bed. After setting his own water on the table, he handed Seb's over. "Here ya go."

Seb, who'd continued to stare at Jared, grabbed his wrist and pulled him onto the bed.

Jared laughed. "Wait. I gotta pee."

He gave Seb a quick kiss before disappearing into the bathroom. Jared stepped up to the toilet and took care of his full bladder. As he stood there, he began to wonder when Seb would make love to him. Surely it would be soon, right? Jared's cock twitched in his hand, liking the idea very much.

When he was almost to the end of his stream, he flushed the stool, shook and stepped to the sink. Damn. No wonder Seb was staring at him earlier. His entire forehead was black and blue, and his hair? *Oh man I need a shower.*

Jared fingered the two butterfly bandages on his face, reminding himself to pick more up at the store. Until he had replacements, he hated to get them wet. He eyed the bathtub. Maybe he could wash his hair without getting his face in the water? Ooh, he thought of a better idea.

He stuck his head out of the bathroom. "I stink. Will you come in and help me wash my hair?"

Seb grinned. "Can I wash your body, too?"

Jared smiled back. "If you'd like."

"Oh, I like," Seb said as he jumped out of bed and grabbed a pair of flannel pyjama pants.

Jared was sad to see the disappearance of his lover's hard cock, but the tub was only big enough for one. He turned on the faucet until the water ran hot and set the plug.

Seb walked into the room and took his turn at the toilet. "I need to call Mac later. Are you sure you're going to feel like working Monday?"

"Of course. Why wouldn't I?" Jared still couldn't believe he'd landed such a dream job. No way would he do something to jeopardise it. He stepped into the tub, hissing as the hot water touched the cuts on his ankles.

"You okay?" Seb asked.

"Yeah. I probably should have done this earlier." Jared slowly lowered himself into the steaming bath.

Seb knelt beside the tub, trailing his fingertips in the water before trickling the warm drops over Jared's arms. "I'm sure Mac would understand if you'd like to take a few days. What you went through…"

"Was a regular day in my old life," Jared finished for him. He reached out and ran his hand over the short bristles of Seb's goatee. "I've figured something out about myself. Despite everything, I'm pretty resilient. Especially now that I know there's more to life than what I was shown in the past."

Seb leaned over the side of the tub and kissed him. "I love you."

It was the sixth time Seb had told him, and Jared knew he'd never tire of hearing it. He still questioned it though and probably would for a long time. On the ride to the police station in Lubbock, he'd even tried to mentally list the positive things about himself Seb could've fallen for. The list just didn't add up to him.

Jared started to lie back in the water, and was quickly supported by Seb with a hand against his back. The hot water against his scalp felt so good he groaned. "That's nice."

"Hmmm, I think I like you like this," Seb said as he soaped a washcloth and rubbed it over the bruises on Jared's chest.

"Bruised?" he asked, confused.

Seb's hand stopped as he stared Jared in the eyes. "No. God, no. I meant wet and naked."

Jared could tell he'd hurt Seb's feelings. He covered Seb's hand. "I'm sorry. I mean, part of me knew that, but…"

"Shhh," Seb soothed. "Let me go get a cup so I can wash your hair."

It was obvious Seb felt uncomfortable about something. Jared wondered if it was what he'd said, the bruises on display, or perhaps the entire situation. He closed his eyes. It was a totally new experience for him to care about someone else's feelings.

The door opened and Seb stepped back inside, cup in hand. One glance at Seb and Jared knew his lover was truly upset. He sat up and turned in the tub to face Seb. "What's wrong?"

"Huh? Nothing." Seb held up the cup. "I just needed this."

Jared leaned his arms on the side of the tub and rested his chin on his hands. "Please talk to me. If I've done something, I need to know what it was."

Seb shook his head. "You haven't. Guess the last twenty-four hours just caught up with me."

Jared knew there was more to it, but their relationship was too new to rock the boat. Although he didn't say anything, Jared gave Seb a knowing look before getting back into position to have his hair washed.

Seb squeezed a good amount of shampoo into his palm before rubbing them together.

Jared closed his eyes as his lover's strong fingers scrubbed and massaged his scalp. He was so into the shampooing, Seb surprised him when he cleared his throat.

"Alexander died of AIDS when he was eight-years-old."

Jared started to turn his head towards Seb, but his lover's hands kept him in place.

"My mom shot heroin her entire pregnancy. It was a wonder Alex survived at all because, like all drug addicts, she didn't care about going to the doctor for prenatal care. She was more concerned with where she'd get her next fix."

"How old were you?" Jared asked.

"I was six when he was born, but I didn't get to see him for almost four months. When my mom went into labour, I didn't know what to do, so I called the police. It was obvious to the paramedics she was using. After Alexander was born, the state made her enter a treatment facility and put me in a foster home. The hospital tried to keep my brother alive through the withdrawals, but he was already infected with the HIV virus."

Seb removed his hands and dunked them into the water. He grabbed the cup from the side of the tub. "Tilt your head back," he instructed.

Jared did as asked, hoping Seb would continue the story.

"When Mom was released she convinced the authorities she was a changed woman. They gave her back me and Alexander." Seb poured the warm water onto Jared's hair, rinsing away the shampoo.

"Of course as soon as the state stopped watching, she went right back to it. That left me to raise Alex. I thought I was doing a pretty good job until it was time for him to start school. I knew he was a lot slower than most kids, but he wanted to go so bad that I told him I'd make it happen. I took him to the free clinic in town because you had to have shots before you could go. That's when I found out the HIV virus had become full-blown AIDS."

Jared couldn't imagine a child trying to deal with a virus some adults couldn't handle. When he didn't feel anymore water being dumped over his head, he opened his eyes. Tears pooled in Seb's eyes as he stared off into space.

"Seb?"

Seb gave his head a slight shake. "Sorry. Lost in my own thoughts there for a second."

"You don't have to talk about this if it makes you sad."

The corner of Seb's mouth tilted upward. "This is the first time I've talked about it. Ever. The clinic called Social Services, they went to my house to talk to mom, found her high as a kite and took me and Alexander away the same day. Because he was classified as special needs, they sent him to a different foster home."

Jared couldn't imagine the two brothers being separated, especially since it sounded like Seb was the one to raise his younger brother.

"They let me see him a couple times over the next three years, but he kept getting sicker and sicker. The last time I saw him was two days before he died." Seb rubbed the moisture from his eyes. "He was mad at me for letting them separate us."

"But you know it wasn't your fault, right? I mean, you were a kid."

Seb nodded. "Part of me knows that now, but at the time I felt I'd betrayed the one person I was put on the earth to protect."

Jared wondered if that was what led Seb into a job of protecting people. "Is that why you're a bodyguard?"

One of Seb's black eyebrows rose. "What?"

"You felt you let your brother down so you're trying to make up for it by protecting the people who hire you." Something suddenly dawned on him. "Is that why you're so protective of me?"

Seb didn't say anything for several moments. He dropped the cup in the water and bowed his head. "Maybe." He took a deep breath and lifted his head. "But that's not why I love you."

Jared stared into Seb's dark eyes. "Why do you love me?"

"Why does the wind blow?" Seb reached out and cupped Jared's cheek. "It's not possible to be around you and not fall in love. After Alexander died, I thought I'd never meet another truly pure soul again, but first I was introduced to Brier, and then he brought you to me."

Jared thought of all the things he'd been through and been made to do over the years. "I love you, but I don't think I deserve you. There's nothing pure about me."

"Bullshit. Men who haven't been through half of what you've endured have become nothing but a product of their environment. Hell, the prisons are full of them. But despite everything, you still have the capacity to see the good in people. That right there is all the proof I need that your past hasn't damaged your soul."

No one had ever made him feel more special than Seb did at that moment. Jared knew he'd die before he ever did anything to prove himself unworthy of Seb's love. "Can I ask you one last question?"

"Sure."

"Will you make love to me for real?"

Seb grinned. "Oh, babe, I make love to you every time I look at you."

"Don't get me wrong, I really like that, but I was hoping for something a little more…physical," he said with a grin.

* * * *

By the time Seb finished washing Jared's hair and carrying him to bed, his lover's stomach had started to growl. "We need to feed you."

Jared pushed the robe off Seb's shoulders. "But first you need to fuck me."

Yeah, he did. Seb had held back as long as he could. The kidnapping had solidified Jared's position in Seb's life.

Seb retrieved the lube and condoms from his bedside drawer and lay down on top of Jared, bracing himself on his forearms. "Promise me you really want this? Because you know I'll give you as long as it takes for you to be sure."

Jared swept the hair out of Seb's face and smoothed it behind Seb's ears. "I've wanted this since the first night we spent together. I thought you were the one who needed time."

Seb grinned. "We both need to work on our communication abilities."

"Agreed. Now, kiss me."

Seb kissed Jared's lower lip before sucking it into his mouth. He swiped the plump flesh with the tip of his tongue and moaned when Jared's legs wrapped around him. Seb had never met a man who got as turned on by kissing as his lover.

He released the swollen lip and sealed his mouth against Jared's. Seb wanted to make sure Jared felt the difference between the things Rick had forced him to do and what Seb was about to do to the man he loved.

As their tongues played an erotic game of charge and retreat, Seb allowed his hands to wander down Jared's bruised but oh-so-soft skin. He broke the kiss and rose up enough to lick a path down Jared's chest. He stopped briefly at Jared's nipples, giving them each attention before moving further south.

Seb made a point to kiss each of the bruises smattered across Jared's torso, willing each of them to heal quickly. With Rick in jail and Bill dead, Seb hoped to never again see another purple and blue mark on the man he loved.

When he came to the long indention leading from Jared's lower stomach to his groin, Seb couldn't resist running his tongue along the sensual trough. Jared moaned, letting Seb know his lover had a sensitive spot. He continued to torment the shallow channel until Jared's erection slapped Seb on the cheek.

Seb glanced up at the grinning man. Taking the hint, Seb enveloped the crown of Jared's cock in his mouth. With his eyes riveted on Jared's facial expressions, Seb set about learning what truly pleased the younger man.

He was thankful Jared didn't bother hiding his reactions to the blowjob. Like most men, it seemed his young lover was most sensitive directly under the head. Seb continued to lap at the long, thin cock as he reached for the lube.

"Do you want to come now or later?" Seb asked as he rubbed some slick around the outside of Jared's hole.

"Both." Jared moaned as Seb slowly inserted the first finger.

"Ambitious." Seb pumped the lone digit in and out of Jared's body, preparing it for a second.

"Young," Jared corrected as Seb introduced the second finger.

Seb's tongue travelled to the wrinkled, but firm sac. He rubbed his goatee gently over the skin between Jared's balls and ass while sucking one of the sensitive orbs into his mouth.

"Uhhh," Jared groaned. He hooked his arms under his knees and opened himself further.

A third finger was introduced, and Seb licked his way back to the head, engulfing as much of Jared's length as he could. The salty taste of his lover's pre-cum clung to his tongue as he allowed Jared to fuck his mouth.

"Oh, shit. It's coming. I'm coming..." Jared broke off on a strangled gasp as the first string of seed hit the back of Seb's throat.

Seb backed off enough to swallow as his mouth was awash with his lover's tangy cum. He licked and kissed Jared's cock clean and reached for the condom. It wasn't until he started to sit up that Seb realised he'd been rubbing and grinding his own cock against the sheets as he'd pleasured Jared.

The realisation that he'd been so focused on giving Jared pleasure that he hadn't noticed his own body's needs, further cemented the changes in himself since he'd met the younger man. In the past, sex had been about one thing. Him getting off.

Seb sat back on his heels and ripped open the foil package. He gazed at his still-recovering lover as he rolled the condom carefully down the length of his erection. Seb knew if he wasn't careful he'd come before even entering the man. How many times had he thought about being buried deep in Jared's ass?

Seb squeezed the base of his dick in an attempt to stave his climax. Jared seemed to notice Seb's predicament and chuckled. "Yeah, keep laughing and your fun will be over, too."

"I'll have to buy you a cock ring," Jared told him while trying to keep a straight face.

The light conversation helped cool his ardour enough to release the hold on his cock. He reached for the lube and applied a generous amount to the condom, using the lightest touch possible.

From the need clearly written on his lover's face, Seb no longer worried it was too soon or Jared was doing it for the wrong reason. He repositioned until the tip of his cock rested against Jared's stretched hole.

With a firm grip on his cock, Seb slowly pushed the thick length of meat through Jared's outer ring of muscles. He wasn't even inside yet and already he could feel the sweat popping out on his forehead as inch by inch Jared's body accepted his girth.

Seb released the hold on his cock and wiped his forehead with his arm. He wondered if fucking Jared would always be this intense. The angelic expression on Jared's face as Seb rocked his way in to the hilt, was something he'd never tire of seeing. There seemed to be such peace on the man's face. Peace, Seb knew, was a long time coming.

"Okay?" he asked.

Jared nodded and squeezed his eyes shut.

The angelic expression turned to something else as Seb withdrew and drove in again. "Am I hurting you?"

Jared opened his eyes. It was then Seb saw the moisture. Seb paused mid-stroke. "Jared? Am I hurting you?"

Jared shook his head. "No. It's wonderful. More than I ever dreamed possible."

Seb leant down and kissed his lover. "You deserve this and so much more. I'm going to spend the rest of my life pleasing you in every way possible."

Jared smiled. "The rest of your life?"

Seb nodded as he braced his weight on his arms, still moving in and out of Jared's passage. "I love you."

"I love you."

With the mushy stuff said, Seb turned his concentration to giving Jared the best orgasm of his life. He knew it was a challenge he'd issue himself every day he and Jared were together.

The squeeze and pull of Jared's velvety walls around his cock was becoming too much to overcome. He knew his climax was closing in on him, but Seb wanted to make sure his lover was fully satisfied first.

"Touch yourself."

Jared grinned and released his hold on one of his legs. Seb took over and positioned both of Jared's legs over his shoulders, giving the man two hands to play.

Jared immediately went to work, pulling and plucking at his light brown nipples. He smiled coyly up at Seb. "Like this?"

Seb's rhythm increased at the playful side of his lover. Although the tableau in front of him was sexy as hell, Seb wanted more. "Let me watch you jack off."

One of Jared's blond eyebrows rose with apparent amusement. He ran one hand down his chest to slap at his bobbing erection. "Like this?"

The sound of Jared's hand slapping against the red and leaking cock, fuelled Seb's ardour further.

He repositioned both of them until most of Jared's weight was resting on his upper back and shoulders. With his feet on the mattress, Seb bent his legs and drove almost straight down in and out of Jared's hole. The new position not only allowed Seb to plunge deeper, but it put Jared's cock almost directly over the younger man's mouth.

Seb alternated his gaze between the hand pumping Jared's cock and his lover's facial expressions. As much as he loved looking down at the vision of erotic play below him, he had to remind himself of Jared's bruised and no doubt sore body.

He'd almost decided it wasn't worth taking the chance of hurting Jared, when the younger man cried Seb's name. As predicted, the strands of opaque fluid shot towards Jared's mouth and face.

Watching Jared move his head to try and catch his own seed pushed Seb over the edge. He came with a ferocity he'd never known, howling Jared's name. Seb fell to his knees and lowered Jared's legs from his shoulders as his body continued to quake. He knew there was a very strong possibility he was about to collapse and hurting Jared wasn't an option.

Although he would have loved to linger inside his lover's body, Seb knew the condom was full to the point of bursting. He wrapped his fingers around the base of the rubber and pulled out.

After a quick knot and toss to the nearby trashcan, Seb fell to the mattress. Still breathing too heavily to speak, he pulled Jared into his arms. *Damn, I love this man.*

Jared was the first to recover. He propped his chin against Seb's chest and gazed up at him. "Is it always like that?"

Seb swallowed, trying to get enough moisture into his throat to speak. "With us? Yeah, I have a feeling it'll be that and more."

"So how many times a day can you do that?" Jared asked.

Seb grinned. "I'm not as young as you are, but I imagine I might be good for twice a day. Will that keep you satisfied? I'd hate to lose you to some other young thing."

Jared slid up Seb's sweaty body to his lips. After an incredibly deep kiss, in which Seb was almost sure he'd received a tonsillectomy, Jared smiled.

"Twice works just fine for me."

Epilogue

"Morning, Brier," Seb said as his friend came into his office.

"Morning." Brier gestured to the chair. "Do you have a minute?"

"Sure. Have a seat." Seb had expected Brier's visit after Rick's conviction the previous morning. Jared's tormenter had been given twenty-three years in the state penitentiary, but he would be eligible for parole in fifteen years.

"Jackie and I were talking about the charges in Oklahoma."

"Yeah?" The prosecutor in Oklahoma had left it up to the victims whether or not they wanted to testify against Rick in a new trial because without their testimony, Oklahoma didn't have a case. The state of Texas had already agreed to extradite Rick to stand trial for the rapes of Brier, Jared and Peter in the mental hospital.

"I still haven't been able to convince Peter to talk, but I want to testify. The thought that Rick could be on the streets in fifteen years scares me," Brier confessed.

It scared Seb as well. There was no doubt in his mind Rick would immediately go after Jared once again upon his release. It didn't matter what face he showed the parole board, Seb knew a monster like Rick would never change. Their best break in the Texas case had been the letters Rick had sent Jared. The fingerprints and handwriting analysis proved Rick had written them, which tied Bill into the case. The prosecutor had used the letters and the kidnapping by Bill to backup Jared's testimony of his time spent at Rick's hands. The jury had been absolutely mortified by the things Jared had been forced to live through at the hands of the two brothers.

"I think that's commendable. I know Jared wants to go through with the trial in Oklahoma. It'll be a lot easier on him this time if you're standing up with him."

Brier nodded. "I was proud of Jared. I know it wasn't easy telling all those people what Rick had done to him, but he did it."

"Yes he did. I think he's changed a lot over the last couple of months," Seb agreed.

Brier stood and stuck his hands in his front pockets. "I'll let you get back to work."

Although Seb really needed to do just that, he couldn't let the moment slip by without issuing an invitation to his friend. "We're having a dinner party at our new place next weekend if you and Jackie would like to come over."

Brier laughed and scratched the top of his head. "Hmmm, well, since it's right next door, I think we could manage that."

Right next door was a little misleading since ten acres separated the two homes, but Seb knew Brier was thrilled to have Jared so close. "Great. You still helping us move on Saturday?"

"You bet."

"Thanks."

Brier nodded and left the office.

Seb sat back in his chair. The home he'd purchased was a little bigger than what they needed, but Jared had been thrilled with the two fireplaces and huge outdoor patio. Seb was happy it was so close to Jackie and Brier. Although his job didn't take him out of town often, he felt better knowing help was close by.

His phone rang, interrupting his train of thought. "Seb James."

"It's Benny Franklin."

"Hi, Mr. Franklin," Seb greeted, rolling his eyes. Keifer Zane's manager had become a major pain in Seb's ass. He knew Benny wasn't happy about his number-one-client's postponement of the tour, but the manager seemed to take his anger out on Seb and he was damned tired of it.

"The tour's back on for next week," Benny told him.

"Yeah. I read about the death of Keifer's mom. I hope you'll please extend my condolences."

"Yeah, sure. Anyway, I was thinking…"

Uh oh.

"Since the whole tour is promoting Keifer's new album, *The Flip Side*, I was thinking maybe your guy, Archer, could dye his hair. He's already rocking the bleached white thing, how about tipping the ends with black? It would make him not only fit in with the theme, but it would make a nice contrast to the white-tipped black hair Keifer's sporting for the tour."

"No," Seb told Benny.

"It's just a little dye. You want your guy to fit in don't you? Isn't the whole point of hiring a gay bodyguard to fool the people into thinking they're really a couple?"

"Listen. Archer's been more than accommodating with this whole situation. He agreed to take only short-term assignments while he waited for Keifer to be with his mom in her final months. But you're crossing the line with this one."

"I can always get another company," Benny threatened.

"Try it. We both know Keifer insisted Archer wait for him to go back on tour. For some reason your client feels safe with my guy, and isn't that the point?"

"Despite what he thinks, Keifer doesn't always call the shots," Benny countered.

"Interesting. Maybe I'll call him and ask what he thinks."

"I've told you before, Keifer doesn't want to think about the business side of his life right now."

"Mmm hmm." Seb didn't buy it for a minute. He had no doubt Keifer would come unglued at the things his manager was spouting. "Look. I've got a million things going on right now. Call me when you have definite details on where and when Archer needs to report for duty."

Before Benny could say anything else, Seb hung up the phone. "Jackass."

* * * *

Seb finished hooking up the computer in his new home office. He looked around at the masculine space and smiled. Never had he imagined he'd own a house so incredibly perfect for him. The library, as it had been advertised, was fabulous. With floor to ceiling bookshelves covering one wall and a huge double window on another, it was as if the architect had had Seb in mind when he'd designed it.

He glanced at the boxes of books he'd ordered in the last month. Finally, he'd be able to buy his favourites instead of rechecking them out from the library constantly. Seb knew it was probably considered wasteful to buy books he'd already read, but for the first time in his entire life, he had a place to store the volumes he loved so much.

As he walked out of the office into the great room, he couldn't wipe the smile off his face. He'd always thought owning a home was a luxury he didn't need. It had always just been him and with his job taking him on the road all the time, he'd never even considered putting down roots to the point of actually buying something.

Jared had changed all that. Seb knew the one thing that would help Jared was a safe, permanent environment. When the house next door to Brier's had gone up for sale, it seemed like it was meant to be. After looking at the house only once, Seb had snapped it up. He'd even paid full price so he wouldn't risk losing the property. He still wasn't sure what he and Jared were going to do with the twenty acres the house sat on though. Brier had suggested a couple of horses, but neither Seb nor Jared was big on horses.

Perhaps they'd get a dog to keep Jelly Bean company once the cat settled into her new surroundings. He entered the kitchen, expecting to find Jared and came up empty. "Jared?"

Seb wandered back through the great room, stopping at the laundry room, before continuing on towards the bedrooms. He found Jared sound asleep in one of the guest rooms. Apparently his lover had been putting sheets on the bed when he'd dropped to the mattress in exhaustion.

It was no wonder. Jared had been up since two that morning. When the alarm had gone off at the ungodly hour, Seb had been surprised when Jared jumped out of bed. Seb had questioned Jared and been informed the dormitory's common room needed to be stripped and waxed.

Seb shook his head and lay on the bed beside his lover. He brushed the blond hair out of Jared's face and grinned at the pouty lips he'd uncovered. Although he'd tried to argue with Jared the common room's floor could wait for another day, Jared wasn't having it.

Jared took his job as serious as any high-powered executive would. He'd informed Seb the floors were looking dull and it was the perfect time to shine them up.

"Baby?" Seb whispered. "Want me to help you to bed?"

Jared whimpered and turned his face away from Seb's voice.

Seb rolled off the bed, and retrieved a heavy down comforter from the bench under the window. He picked the pillows up from the same bench and made the bed around Jared's sleeping form.

Jared was so worn out he didn't even stir when Seb undressed him and tucked him under the covers. Seb gave Jared a kiss on the forehead and walked back into the great room.

He noticed his flashing cell phone when he walked past the coffee table and picked it up. He plopped down on the couch and began reading the text message from Archer.

On my way to Philli to meet up with Jimmy. What the hell is this shit about me colouring my hair. Fix this, Seb, or someone's going 2 die.

Seb hit speed dial and waited.

"Hey," Archer answered.

"Don't worry about the hair thing. I've already told Benny to go fuck himself over that," Seb tried to put Archer's mind at ease.

"So whose idea was it in the first place? Because Benny's trying to tell me Jimmy plans to fire me if I don't follow orders. And you and I both know I don't deal with shit like that. If Jimmy wants to play that way, he can damn-well find another sucker to play dress-up with him."

"Relax. It wasn't Jimmy, it was Benny. Let me call Jimmy directly and see if we can't work this out. I've had my fill of Benny as well."

"Thanks, boss."

"Yeah, just keep the wackos away from Jimmy and I'll be happy," Seb told him.

"I can do that as long as I don't have to deal with his asshole manager."

"You and me both. I'll call you back if I can get hold of Jimmy." Seb ended the call. He scrolled down in his list of contacts and brought up Jimmy Cook AKA Keifer Zane and punched it in.

The phone rang five times before a scratchy voice answered. "Zane."

"Jimmy, it's Seb James. Sorry to hear about your mom."

"Thanks, Mr. James."

"Call me Seb. Anyway, Archer's on his way to meet you in Philadelphia."

"That's good."

"Yeah, well, he's having a few issues with your manager," Seb informed the superstar.

"Fuck. What's Benny done now?"

"He wants Archer to dye his hair. And quite frankly, we're both tired of dealing with his shit. I know you need him and everything, but we don't. I'd like to deal directly with you instead of Benny."

"And Archer feels the same way?" Jimmy asked.

"Yeah. Actually, I think Archer mentioned something about bodily harm if Benny tries to fuck with him again."

Jimmy chuckled. "Have you ever seen Benny? I might pay good money to see that battle."

Although Seb had never met Benny, he'd seen his picture in several magazine articles. Jimmy was no shorty, coming in at nearly five foot eleven, but Benny Franklin had to stand at least six-six and that was without the trademark black bowler hat he always wore. At close to three hundred pounds, Benny intimidated a lot of people. Fortunately Seb and Archer weren't among them.

"Don't let Archer's size fool you. He's more than capable of taking on anyone who stands in his way. I wouldn't have assigned him to you if I didn't think he was the perfect man for the job," Seb explained.

"Oh, I've no doubt Archer could kick Benny's ass which is why I would pay good money to see it," Jimmy said around a chuckle. "I know I wouldn't be half as successful without Benny, but he does have a tendency to try and push people around."

"Yeah, well, as long as Benny understands Archer won't be playing his games or answering to him everything should go smoothly."

"I'll talk to him," Jimmy agreed.

"Thanks, and good luck with the tour."

"Six months on the road isn't my idea of a good time, but it helps pay for the other six months of the year."

Seb ended the call and immediately got in touch with Archer. He told Archer about his conversation with Jimmy before hanging up. Seb turned off his phone and tossed it back onto the table. He systematically checked the doors and turned off the lights as he wound his way back towards the guest room.

Jared was still asleep. He'd even started the soft snore Seb thought was so damn cute.

Seb undressed and crawled under the covers. He spooned his body against Jared's and kissed the younger man's neck. All day he'd looked forward to sleeping in the big new bed he and Jared had picked out, but evidently it wasn't going to happen.

There was no way he wanted to wake his sleeping lover, and as he'd promised months ago, wherever Jared went, Seb would always be right there with him.

About the Author

An avid reader for years, one day Carol Lynne decided to write her own brand of erotic romance. Carol juggles between being a full-time mother and a full-time writer. These days, you can usually find Carol either cleaning jelly out of the carpet or nestled in her favourite chair writing steamy love scenes.

Carol loves to hear from readers. You can find her contact information, website details and author profile page at http://www.total-e-bound.com

Total-E-Bound Publishing

www.total-e-bound.com

Take a look at our exciting range of literagasmic™
erotic romance titles and discover pure quality
at Total-E-Bound.